THE RIPPLE EFFECT

Lyz Harvey

Bloomington, IN Milton Keynes, UK

authorHOUSE®

AuthorHouse™
1663 Liberty Drive, Suite 200
Bloomington, IN 47403
www.authorhouse.com
Phone: 1-800-839-8640

AuthorHouse™ UK Ltd.
500 Avebury Boulevard
Central Milton Keynes, MK9 2BE
www.authorhouse.co.uk
Phone: 08001974150

First published by AuthorHouse 4/20/2007

ISBN: 978-1-4259-9638-3 (sc)

Printed in the United States of America
Bloomington, Indiana

This book is printed on acid-free paper.

Ripples impinging,

intersecting as they spread,

incalculably

With my love and thanks

to all those whose effects have rippled - through me,

then on to countless others ...

�功✶

→1←

THE SECRETARY BREATHED A SIGH of relief.

"I'll swing for that woman one of these days" she muttered under her breath, watching from behind the curtains as the Chairwoman and the other two cronies departed, making their way to where George awaited his employer, holding the car door open.

Turning to Elsie, an amiable sort who let nothing upset her on principle, and Janet, who would not say 'boo' to the proverbial goose, she looked from one to the other.

"What do you propose doing about *that*, then?"

"There's nothing we *can* do, Margaret," replied Janet "we'll have to amend the constitution, as she said."

"But we're the ones who have to bear the brunt of the complaints, and it's so *unfair*."

"She's within her rights, I suppose" ventured Elsie "being Chairwoman and having the casting vote and all that, but it's always the same - she invariably manages to get her own way."

" ... and all I can do is put it in the minutes as proposed and carried – just because she had her friends here. We never see them when we want some practical help with the fundraising."

"Well, if it's any comfort, it's not just *our* Committee."

Disconsolately they started to gather the coffee cups and biscuits.

Lady Sonia of Woolston Manor had deigned to nod haughty acknowledgement to her two acquaintances, their roles having been played so that she had again won the day, and sat back in her car with an irritated air as the chauffeur arranged the rug over her lap. Village life is becoming so

1

tiresome, she thought. However, she saw it as her duty to direct those who would otherwise get bogged down by their own incompetence – and duty was something she had certainly never shirked.

Perhaps in the New Year she would revise her schedule and stand down from the most boring committees. She had set a standard, after all, and surely they could continue without her, providing they followed her precedents. As one's years advanced, being a pillar of the community was somewhat of a mixed blessing. Tapping George on the shoulder, she directed him to drive to Guildford – she would spend half an hour at the small gallery she had recently decided to patronise. There was always room at the Hall for another local watercolour of quality.

George, knowing which side his bread was buttered, had long ago cultivated an expressionless response, and respectfully murmured "Yes, m'lady" as all good chauffeurs are trained to do, and resigned himself to missing coffee and chat in the kitchen with Annie and Doris.

It was, to outward appearances at least, just like any other day at Woolston Hall, and, apart from the extra preparations for Lady Sonia's birthday in the following month, the planned changes that would be taking place gave no hint of the cataclysmic upheavals to come from the unplanned ones.

She, Lady Sonia that is, had decided it was to be a celebration reminiscent of years long past, when the Hall was the focal point of so many business calendars and invitations were much-coveted accolades of success. Preparations for *this* event, Lady Sonia's 70th birthday (to be celebrated by all and sundry, like it or not, on Christmas Day - no matter how inconvenient) had begun in October, with lists of guests and food, programmes of shopping and ordering. Every taste catered for, every eventuality covered even before it might be thought of as a problem - aspects of hospitality for which the Hall had become renowned in Sir Geoffrey's time.

Annie emerged from the pantry with yet another armful of ingredients. "What is it this time?"

"Florentines. I've been drying the tins ready to store them."

Doris paused, hands on hips, arching her aching back, then wiping a wisp of hair from her brow with the back of a hand. She was the epitome of the old-fashioned middle-aged cook-housekeeper, surveying the scene in the kitchen with a practised eye. The kitchen was undoubtedly the hub of the household, jealously guarded by Doris as her domain, and she deferred only to Lady Sonia who, as her employer, was the only one allowed to voice opinions. It was an empire to be proud of and with standards to be maintained zealously.

"I shall be glad when that girl from the village starts. Work Experience I think they're calling it. Well, she'll get plenty of experience here for a couple of weeks. Enough to put her off work for life, maybe."

"Think of all the experiences we've had, and we're still part and parcel of the Hall ..." mused Annie, pouring mugs of tea for the two of them. "Come on, it's ten-thirty, and we can have this before you start mixing. Let's have a look at the paper for a few minutes, then I can start the coffee for upstairs when her ladyship returns."

They settled into companionable silence for what had become their morning ritual in the past few years since the regime at the Hall had changed. Doris's mind was full of today's list – after the Florentines, she would start mince pies. Dundee cakes were already wrapped in greaseproof paper and stored, and the heavy fruit birthday cake was upside down in its container, halfway through the daily spoonfuls of brandy that prepared it for the later layers of marzipan and icing.

The notice board in the kitchen was full of different handwritten lists, carefully arranged in sequence, equally carefully adhered to, ticked and filed away - a system that had worked well when the Hall was in its heyday. Doris was glad she had retained them – it made life easier now she was a little, well, more mature. Methodical, reliable, unflappable, she had needed all those qualities to survive Lady Sonia for so long. The mainstay of the domestic scene, her lack of further ambition had been exploited for more years than she cared to remember, but she cherished and totally believed a conversation once held many years ago when Lady Sonia had been recovering from an illness that had meant a short stay in hospital.

"The food was certainly not to my taste, and I just couldn't wait to get back to my own home, Doris. Stay in my service and you'll never want for anything for the rest of your life."

Well, there were definitions of what Doris might want that changed over the years, but she saw no reason to doubt those words and the intention behind them. On the whole she had been happy enough - at least until recently. Now, however, the order of things had definitely changed and showed worrying signs of becoming unbearable, no matter what incentive there might be to stay on.

The problems centred around Benjamin's wife of course, Lady Sonia's new daughter-in-law, and were especially worrying when Victoria (whenever her indomitable mother-in-law was out of the way) tried to insist on reorganising minor domestic matters that had been running perfectly smoothly for years

- under the pretext of 'updating'. Doris had already come very close to telling her employer that she could not be expected to work for two mistresses.

Doris rose, with effort, and resumed her place at the other end of the table, checking the assorted ingredients. Annie looked up at the clock, folded the paper, hastily drank the last of her tea and started to assemble the coffee tray. Small and neat, she darted around the kitchen. Hanging her apron behind the door, she glanced in the mirror, patting a strand of her faded auburn hair now streaked with grey. Whatever happened to the real Annabel Waite, she wondered, as a reflection of a stranger looked back at her from the glass – where was the girl who had once been so happy? Sometimes her life had seemed to consist solely of different performances, the current one of "devoted Lady's companion" had definitely been the most demanding, and so lengthy that she had almost forgotten who her real self might be. A small shiver made her turn away from her reflection and back to the task in hand.

The Hall occupied a significant part of the Surrey countryside - near enough to Guildford to be convenient, yet distant enough from the M25 to feel completely rural. The last two miles from the nearest motorway junction wound through smaller lanes to bring the traveller to the village then beyond, to large wrought iron gates set in a semicircular sweep of rich red brickwork, bound and capped by Portland stone to match the style of the Hall. The Lodge, set back slightly from the driveway just inside the gates, no longer needed to perform its original function of gatehouse; modern communication linked the intercom by the stone pillar with the big house.

The landscaping of the nineteenth century had favoured an avenue of limes leading to the well-kept grounds surrounding the house. A slight curve in the drive led to an air of mystery about what lay ahead. In late spring, with high banks of rhododendrons providing a backdrop behind the newly-leaved trees, it was an approach probably at its best - but even in winter when the bare trunks and branches were starkly outlined against the dark shrubbery, it had a grace and beauty.

The Hall was a very distinct example of its time. The gateway had echoed this, but older and more mellowed red bricks formed the main square building with single storey wings at each side; gables rose at the front, outlined with stonework in an enthusiastic tribute to the architect's whim; imposing bay windows jutted their solid shapes, and crenellations against the contrasting brick and drainpipes formed exclamation marks, emphasising corners protected by more stonework.

The garden boundaries were marked by a profusion of stone urns. Long-established walkways with herbaceous borders meandered through the grounds, punctuated by statuary. The gardens had always been a significant part of the charm of the Hall, particularly in the days when Sir Geoffrey was in his heyday. To be invited to the house parties was an honour, and greatly appreciated by other businessmen. Grottos and nooks were the scene of many a deal being conducted in the utmost privacy. More 'personal' usage was also a feature, but discreetly so of course, with never a hint of scandal reaching the ears of Lady Sonia – it was essential to protect good standing with the couple, to say nothing of blighting potential business opportunities.

Wheeling the coffee trolley into the drawing room, Annie paused just before her usual discreet tap at the half open door. She could hear Lady Sonia's authoritative tones from the far end of the room, as she explained yet another nuance of essential etiquette to the hapless Victoria.

Sharply featured, elegantly dressed and immaculately groomed, her Ladyship sat straightbacked and formal at her writing desk with a pile of lists, giving total concentration to the task in hand. Her hands were slim claws, bearing the weight of several heavy diamond rings of flawless quality, matched by discreet diamond studs in her ears. She had taken care to ensure that hallmarks of quality and value had emphasised her improvements in life at every turn, and years of practice had honed her air of good breeding, so that she truly appeared to be "to the manner born", with not a trace of the flatter vowels of her provincial upbringing ever betraying her origins - of which, of course, she never spoke. With the wealth and standing she had acquired ensuring that she carried weight in the levels of the community she chose to honour with her presence, she had chosen committee work wisely. Significant enough to be household names, yet offering duties not too onerous to be fitted into the demands of providing the correct setting at the Hall to give the perfect backdrop for the business deals, charity work fitted well into forming a list of significant contacts. Sonia understood well what made the wheels of her world go round, but was not too bound up in the work to weigh up its usefulness, and the village could well do without her time from now on. But confirmation of her thoughts could be left until the New Year – it was time now to concentrate on the matter in hand.

Vicky, sitting at her side, looked totally bored – alert enough only to become artificially animated when her mother-in-law turned to her for confirmation that she understood a particular point. Her seventh month of pregnancy did not suit her at all. She had none of the bloom that sometimes happens even after a difficult first trimester, and her sallow skin appeared out of condition, as did her short dark hair, listlessly flopping forward into her eyes and needing constant flicks into place behind her ears.

A young woman given to sulkiness, a pout her almost constant expression these days, she shared none of the joyful anticipation that her pregnancy seemed to bring to her husband and his mother. Their expectations of a son, and the continuity of a dynasty that had long been planned by Sonia and her late husband, and on this matter they were completely blinkered. Only once, soon after she suspected she was pregnant, had Vicky wondered whether to point out that it might not be a boy, but she had adamantly refused the information when it was offered later by the doctors, just in case Ben chose to use it as an excuse not to marry her. Vicky's ambition was almost as ruthless as her future mother-in-law's had been at her age, and it would be soon enough to face that hurdle when the child was born.

But Vicky felt cheated. She had intended to have at least a few years of getting accustomed to the new life she had married into, and seeing what she could get from it, before deciding whether motherhood was for her or not. There was no doubt that she would eventually have persuaded Ben that they should marry - he was besotted by her, and she knew just how to keep him interested, but the unexpected pregnancy had hastened the wedding – and even in the first years of the new millennium some old-fashioned values still lingered on in families where outward appearances predominated. The wedding had not been quite the lavish society affair she had craved, but grand enough to make some of her erstwhile friends envious, and she had decided that life in Ben's private rooms at the Hall would be worth any inconvenience of living under the same roof as his mother.

Unfortunately, she had found that once she was married her role had subtly but swiftly changed from that of the cherished love of Ben's life, to becoming an understudy for Ben's adored mother. Why had she not seen the warning signs sooner, she was to ask herself increasingly as time passed.

Sonia was a force with a momentum so powerful that no scope for anything other than acquiescence was possible, and Vicky, young enough to wish to assert her independence, yet unskilled in knowing the ways and means that might achieve it, had to bow to her mother-in-law's wishes at all times. It had hurt that Ben had taken his mother's side in all differences of opinion, and it was only the thought of their eventual inheritance of the Hall that prevented more stubbornness on Vicky's part. She learned to play her part, but grudgingly, and inevitably the mantle of resentment began to fall on her in a grey cloud of depression. All she could do was keep her hopes projected forward to a time when her manipulative mother-in-law's powers would inevitably fade.

Annie was about to withdraw discreetly from the drawing room when Sonia's imperious tones made her obediently turn back.

"Tell George I shall need the car after all, Annie – sharp at 2 o'clock. He will be taking us to Guildford."

Annie, with years of practice, betrayed no reaction to the command other than a respectful nod of acquiescence. No use explaining that it was George's afternoon off duty, no use trying to tell Sonia that George had made plans to take his mother for a birthday treat. Sonia had spoken. Sonia must be obeyed. Not surprisingly, chauffeurs came and went fairly rapidly after Sir Geoffrey's death, unable to cope with the unfeeling demands of his widow. Sonia decided not to notice the faint stiffening of Annie's posture. She knew full well it was George's free afternoon, but sometimes chose to remind employees that their employer was in control. It felt good to be in charge of people's lives.

"You may pour the coffee Victoria." Sonia never used the diminutive. The girl was looking pasty again. Such a pity that today's young women went to pieces. Pregnancy was a natural process, for Heaven's sake, but at this rate it would be not a moment too soon when the waiting was over.

Sonia turned to the guest list again, checking the three sections – house guests, visiting family and close friends, and expected villagers and local contacts.

"The success of any function on this scale depends on meticulous planning, and imparting to the guests a thorough understanding of their participation. In that way, everyone is clear about what we expect from them - departure times are just as important as when they arrive."

Vicky handed Sonia her coffee. She knew that she was being groomed for a time when she would be expected to take over these duties - under Sonia's watchful eye at first of course, then eventually she would be trusted on her own. It could take years, but while Sonia was still around Vicky could not expect to be allowed a free rein. It was proving to be a more difficult role than she had envisaged, but the rewards were so great that she had rationalised it to herself as a learning and qualifying process – her Master's degree in Mistress-ship, as she had once described it to a friend in an unusual moment of levity.

Vicky was not renowned for her wit or sense of humour.

Downstairs again, Annie sighed as she picked up the house phone to speak to George. Doris stopped chopping the nuts for the Florentines. Hearing Annie's part of the conversation, she gestured in sympathy. Poor George. How long would *he* continue to bite his lip and endure the treatment? True, Sonia had an amazing ability to keep some employees longer than would have been thought possible, but it seemed to have more to do with the employees' needs for a job than their conditions of work.

<h1 style="text-align:center">⇢2⇠</h1>

Barbara looked again at the invitation as dusk fell. How many more gatherings would she attend, she mused, pouring another large gin, and splashing a token amount of tonic into the antique cut glass tumbler.

As Sonia's oldest friend she had been honoured by a handwritten letter, outlining her expected part in the preparations – three days prior to the birthday her usual room would be available. Inwardly she sometimes felt manipulated, but outwardly she always took care to co-operate with whatever arrangements Sonia chose to make, however inconvenient it might be to her own private schedule. It had paid dividends in the past and, after all, she did have a genuine fondness for her friend after the long years of seeing Sonia make the most of her own opportunities in life. In fact, Barbara had learned a great deal over the years, and her own achievements made life more comfortable in ways she could never have foreseen when they first met, had there not been the background of the Hall from which to make the contacts on which her comfortable position in life rested.

It was certainly a long way from the drab house she had called home, in the drab post-war town where they had both attended the same school - although four years difference in age had meant that they did not actually form any friendship until later, meeting at a time when they briefly worked in the same office. Sonia had left to further her prospects, Barbara had stayed for a while, but they did not lose touch, as, apart from the common bonds of school and training, they had discovered a similarity of background. Barbara's openness had enabled Sonia to confide in someone for the first time in her life, and although Barbara had not had to suffer the stigma of a father who left her mother for another woman, she herself had lived without a father from the age of twelve, trying to absorb her own widowed mother's grief. Having exchanged their experiences at that early age, it was a measure of Sonia's trust that she knew she could rely on Barbara's discretion, and nothing ever went further than their own private conversations.

Strange how life turned out, Barbara thought, glancing around the opulence of her flat, relishing the contrast between the 'then and now' of her life. Who would have thought that a girl from her ordinary background would have reached such a pinnacle of comfort? Once having decided that her destined path in life had little to do with the shorthand skills in which she had trained, but everything to do with her own brand of public relations, she accepted her clients good advice and generosity, and had earned the essential London base many years ago. Had she been given to introspection she might have linked the missing father figure in her life with her own readiness to accept favours. However, it was one part of herself that she successfully kept hidden from Sonia, knowing that Sonia was capable of a cold ruthlessness that would end even the oldest friendship if it were deemed necessary. Sonia, for her part, never gave it a thought. As she never went to Barbara's flat, and their only contact was when Barbara's assistance was needed for conferences, she was best left in ignorance.

Other parts of Chiswick had changed, but this had been a good investment and would most probably always be regarded as the better area, close to the park yet within easy reach of the High Road. Barbara looked round the room and smiled fondly; she was pleased with her taste in this high ceilinged room with its elaborate cornices and period marble fireplace. On the wall opposite the tall sash windows the Georgian glass fronted cabinets reflected the lessening glow of the setting sun, their displays of delicate porcelain figurines shown to best advantage within the frame of burnished mahogany. On the mantelpiece an exquisite gilded Louis Quinze clock took pride of place; a jeweller's display case contained so many small delights of gems and miniature gold charms nestling cheek by jowl with a few Faberge pieces. Whichever direction one looked there were delights, and everything contained so many memories of so many rewarding times.

Barbara drew the heavy velvet floor length drapes. These days she loved the onset of winter and the excuse to retreat into 'hibernation mode' – her only concession to her sixty-six years. Another party at the Hall – well, it would be a date not to miss, and would give her a chance to meet Benjamin's wife again.

What *was* her name … oh, Victoria, that's right. Such a scheming little minx she'd appeared to be at first, but Sonia would carry on training her well, and would, no doubt, get her to a stage of being a worthy successor. Sonia had seen potential in her and had encouraged her beloved Benjamin to settle down. When he showed reluctance she had even thought of suggesting to her prospective daughter-in-law that the age-old ploy of feigned pregnancy might be used, she had once confided in Barbara. Fortunately nature took matters into its own hands, and although the result was a hastier entry into married life than any of the concerned parties had hoped, nonetheless it all showed signs of great promise under the ever watchful eye of the mistress of the Hall. Barbara settled into her chair with the footstool, a table just large enough to hold the latest novel she was reading, ash-tray, bottle and the tall crystal glass. Time to relish the thought of the forthcoming Christmas Day that promised to be like no other …

Jacqueline's preparations for Christmas ground relentlessly on, but she enjoyed it more this year than for as long as she could remember. She had relaxed into her marriage now and had confidence in the feelings that had proved themselves well-founded. At first it had seemed incredible that any man had even shown the slightest genuine interest in her.

"A twice-married thirty-something with two children by different fathers" was her flippant self-deprecating comment when Richard once asked her how she would describe herself, but was taken aback by his vehement response.

"Don't *ever* put yourself down like that – *I* see a woman of courage and great depths, and I know you'll be capable of achieving anything you set your mind to."

Oh, he was the most perfect man for her, and she had daily reminders that this was so. It was not because he had so rapidly started to tell her of his conviction that he wanted her in his life forever, but he was prepared to wait until she was ready for him, no matter how long it took. With this emotional security obvious and available, Jacqui was ready far sooner than she had anticipated after the events of the previous years. The longer she knew him, the more Richard proved rock solid and supportive without being over-protective. Soon she could no longer imagine life without him, and they slipped away one weekend to a quiet wedding that had none of the publicity her first had attracted, nor any of the mixed feelings of her second. Any doubts, she realised, had largely been due to anticipating her mother's disapproval of what she would, no doubt, see as only a slightly more acceptable husband than the first had been.

Sonia, of course, had very fixed ideas of who was suitable for either of her twins, and Richard would have been better advised to have turned up first in Jacqueline's life – it would have saved much heartache and bitter feelings. But timing is everything and at least he had come on the scene at a time when Jacqui could appreciate his qualities, and she was able to announce their wedding to Sonia - although only after it had taken place.

While Richard was busy establishing his past as junior partner in the country medical practice, Jacqui was able to care full-time for Tim and Ella. They planned to have their own child at a later date, but there was no need to hurry – let the two older ones settle into the reassuring normality of their newly formed family life, and forget the traumas of the past; she was thankful that even having Sonia as mother-in-law had not daunted Richard from marrying.

"You must take no notice of how she treats me," she had said as they travelled to the Hall for the first time as a family "it's something I can cope with, so please let me deal with it in my own way."

Richard said little, but inevitably noticed Sonia's obvious preference for her son, and what could only be described as a barely tolerant indifference to her daughter. However, Jacqui's relationship with Ben was loving and warm, as was to be expected from a twin sister, and she offset his tendency to be a 'Mother's boy' very well. A succession of girlfriends through the years had been expected by Sir Geoffrey, his late father, and the subject of many references to Benjamin being a 'chip off the old block' and other innuendos – well out of earshot of his wife, of course.

Sonia's attitude had been that she tolerated rather than welcomed the prospect of another woman in her son's life, and vetted them all for suitability of class, financial background (gold-diggers abounded in some circles) and potential succession to herself. Her reactions were invariably heeded – which did not mean to say that her precious Benjamin encountered only the pure and suitable girls his mother wanted, but he soon learned that there was a vast difference between the sort of girlfriends he could bring home to meet the family, and the ones with whom he could have active and non-meaningful relationships. In other words, the normal way of life for those young men with whom he had rubbed shoulders at school and through his undistinguished time at University.

Jacqueline met a few of them, and warmed to some more than others, naturally, but became less involved as her own life produced its significant demands of marriage at a young age. Ben had clumsily offered support, but had been unable to offer any practical help with either her divorce from Zak, or during her bereavement after Anthony's death - his loyalty to their mother getting in the way of his natural feelings.

Time passed, and as Jacqui became less in touch with her brother due to the twists and turns of her own life, she had not been party to the early stages of Ben's relationship with Victoria. In fact, due to the circumstances, she was only introduced just before the imminent wedding was announced at the informal betrothal dinner at the Hall, where she sat quietly wishing above all that their father could be at her side. Shortly after the wedding, when she discovered that the haste was due to Victoria's pregnancy, she offered friendship, as was natural between sisters-in-law and as a mother to a mother-to-be, but received little by way of warmth and responsiveness from the bride.

At the time of Sonia's seventieth birthday Ben had been married for less than six months, and it was not turning out at all as he had expected. He had always found Vicky to be moody, even more so now she was pregnant, but he expected her new way of life to provide a welcome distraction from her physical condition. Sometimes he wished that he had not been so stupid as to rush into the marriage - but having confided his predicament to his mother when Victoria had announced her pregnancy, Sonia had seized the opportunity to gain a daughter-in-law who at least appeared to have the potential to be trained for her position at the Hall. The pregnancy was a bonus, and the expectation that Sonia would soon have a grandson was uppermost in her mind when she firmly told her son that it most definitely was the right time for him to settle down and produce the next generation of Woolstons.

Ben had acquiesced readily enough. He was tired of playing the field, felt sufficient emotional attachment to Vicky to sustain a permanent relationship, and vaguely thought that everything would settle down without too much effort from himself. When the marriage developed early teething troubles as all marriages can, it was unfortunate that it was Lady Sonia in whom he confided. Sonia, also unfortunately, appeared to relish this, welcoming the knowledge that her son had not left her, and that she was still the prime love in his life.

Jacqui observed all this intermittently from the sidelines, but realising she was unable to do anything to improve the situation, wisely kept her thoughts to herself. Yet she felt sad that her brother could not have the easy and rewarding fulfilment that she and Richard had. It was Jacqueline's nature to want everyone to have good things in their lives, and to help people discover what they might be. She had touched on that happiness and fulfilment with Anthony, her second husband, then had it snatched away by the accident. Now she had a second chance with Richard – life was good, and she knew how to value and cherish the quality of their love for each other.

But now it was Christmas Day – and not only that, but also Sonia's birthday celebrations. The car sped along the roads towards the Hall. It would only be a thirty-minute journey with no commuters on the motorway at this time of day. The children sat in the back seat, half-dozing after the excitement of the previous evening's anticipation, then the ritual of sleepily rousing, feeling the weight of a full Christmas stocking on their beds, and contentedly murmuring "he's been!" before shuffling back into cosy happiness for the second part of the night's sleep.

This year, of course, it was to be a different Christmas Day. The normal routine was to travel to Woolston Hall in time for lunch with their grandmother. Sonia's personal habit was always to rise early to attend morning service in the village church with Benjamin, then return to the Hall, where Jacqueline's arrival with the children would coincide with drinks before lunch, and gifts would be exchanged in the drawing room. With the Christmas tree set up away from the fire, and painstakingly trimmed by Doris and Annie with festoons of tinsel, strings of lights, and fascinating miniature toys hanging from every available branch, it was instant Christmas wonderment.

Jacqui had cherished the moment last year when Tim and Ella, eyes shining, stepped into the drawing room and saw the 'magic tree' as Tim had always called it, with neat piles of parcels around the foot. They were carrying Granny's birthday presents and rushed in, insisting on giving them to her even before they had taken off coats and mittens.

Whatever Sonia thought of her daughter in private, she had the grace to put on sufficient pretence in front of the children. Welcoming them with a somewhat formal peck on each cheek, and after accepting their gifts, she asked what Father Christmas had brought. Tim had proudly showed her his new watch and had been asked to "Tell Granny what time it is".

Saving him from the embarrassment of having to admit that he had not yet learned how to do that, his sister Ella came toddling up to Nonny, as she insisted on calling her grandmother;

"Nonny, look!" waving a doll destined to be her favourite toy of all time, a creature of lurid coloured clothes, brown limbs and face. Sonia flinched, but forced a brave smile as the flailing limbs threatened to dislodge her spectacles. Sonia had, from her birth, felt strangely drawn to the child – an unexpectedly emotional bond that she had never felt after her own pregnancy. Not that it resulted in anything other than a slightly warmer response than she afforded their mother. Anything more would have been seen as a sign of weakness, and she was the last person to encourage closeness that could lead the way to over-familiarity in any form.

"Oh … lovely, dear, now do be careful …."

Jacqui retrieved her daughter and led her to look again at the tree.

"When Mummy was a little girl like you, Uncle Ben and I always helped put the decorations on the tree. See that little glass trumpet? It's ever so old. And the glass balls with the crinkly edges? – they belonged to *my* granny."

The small girl had stood, finger in mouth, trying to think of her Mummy as very little – gave up the task and squatted to look at the packages in their Christmas paper with bows. Soon both children were engrossed in the presents.

That was last year. This year, of course, Sonia's birthday party was to eclipse any routine Christmas celebrations - the family would be part of a very much larger gathering. Richard knew how much effort his wife put into maintaining the link between the children and her mother, and how she hoped that one day the children would be able to achieve what she herself had not, and a better relationship would result.

Sonia was not a naturally affectionate woman, but Jacqui ensured that Granny was part of daily conversations at home, even though the children saw her only a few times each year, mostly to commemorate birthdays. She herself made a weekly telephone call to her mother, always including the children, with a piece of news they could 'tell Granny'. Sometimes Sonia appeared to be responsive and Jacqui would raise her hopes that one day their relationship would become easier. As ever, her mother's usual vacillation between what appeared to be indifference and animosity was puzzling.

Jacqui had sat back in the car seat as they drove to the Hall, musing about her life. She had grown up in the knowledge that her twin brother Ben was Sonia's favoured one, and indeed had never questioned it. Her father's his love for both his children included a special element for his daughter, which provided compensation for what his wife could not. It seemed, if not entirely natural, an arrangement that at least appeared to preserve a balance in the family.

Jacqui's second husband Anthony, the hypnotherapist and father of Timmy, had had his own theories, but could do nothing except sustain Jacqui's faith in her own beliefs that one day Sonia would somehow warm to her daughter. Experienced and skilful in picking up clues, Anthony suspected that there was an area of Sonia's life that no-one knew about. He'd already seen how secretive she could be about events that did not add to the image of perfection she decided her life had to be – even to the point of denying illness. A chauffeur had once made the mistake of referring to a visit to a private clinic that had been made. Sonia overheard the remark as she entered the kitchen to give orders to Doreen, and saw this as a gross betrayal of trust. Her tirade led to his dismissal, which was to be expected - and when she had to have regular treatment for a few months, she told no-one anything other than that she was "going into town for a shopping spree", which would necessitate staying overnight then having a few day's rest when she returned home.

Anthony had never had the chance to get further than the suspicions about Sonia's past – perhaps as well, Jacqui sometimes thought – she had noticed that those who tried to come too close to her mother would not last long as friends. Barbara was the only one who had survived as Sonia's confidante, and being the soul of tact that she was, had managed to steer a tricky route of maintaining that friendship, but also being a favourite person in Jacqui's life, too. Anthony's car accident after only months of marriage was a tragic blow, and Jacqui had to concentrate all her energies on the pregnancy Anthony never had a chance to know.

Then came Ella's birth and her own subsequent life as a single mother. It was Barbara, her mother's friend, who stepped in and gave most comfort to Jacqui in those terribly bewildering months.

Jaqui shivered slightly at the memory and firmly told herself to concentrate on the day of celebrations ahead.

﹖3﹖

SONIA HAD SPENT AN HOUR after attending the morning service at the church, dictating and dominating (her two favourite pastimes), and receiving several satisfactory telephone congratulations on achieving her three score years and ten. A late breakfast had been served for all those in the house, as the buffet would be available for the afternoon party, then the family evening meal would take place once all the visitors had left.

After breakfast, dignified enthusiasm had greeted Benjamin's disclosure that he had ordered seventy rose bushes, to be planted at the appropriate time. As an immediate gift, he had bought his mother an exquisite gold bracelet set with rubies, that Victoria had chosen. They both basked in her favour. Barbara had triumphed again with her traditional gift of handmade Swiss chocolates, and this year to commemorate her friend's special birthday, a dainty pair of antique silver sweet tongs to complement them.

Annie and Doris went to the large dining room with Lisa, putting the final touches to the buffet, checking the various flower arrangements, making sure the glasses were sparkling – part of what was once their usual house party routine from years ago, when a buffet would be provided for the guests on the day of departure. Lisa, just fifteen, and experiencing her first time at the Hall, was terrified of Sonia, and very nervous, but proud to have been chosen - Sonia chaired the School Governor Committee, so the Head Teacher had known how imperative it would be for him to select the right girl for the occasion. Lisa's neat hair and carefully discreet makeup perfectly set off the formal uniform of black skirt and white blouse, and she looked far more mature than her years. Benjamin had already noticed her, thought Annie, more attuned to those things than Doris, and she determined to keep a discreet eye on the girl – the last thing they needed would be any scandal, and Annie's deep mistrust of men guided her protective instincts.

Vicky had been ordered to attend Sonia's preparations before the gathering, scheduled for 3 o'clock, began. They made their way slowly up the wide staircase an hour before the first guests could be expected, even Sonia's dignified pace slowing to match Victoria's eighth month pregnancy need. It was her only concession these days to the expected arrival of her grandchild. She had been more irritated than she cared to disclose by Victoria's 'below par' pregnancy, and hoped that it would soon pass when the child was born. The nursery had been prepared well in advance, in a room that was part of Benjamin's suite, and fortunately well out of earshot of Sonia's rooms. The child would be part of the family when she, Sonia permitted – with none of that over-familiarity that seemed to be encouraged these days.

It would be too tiresome if Victoria became a doting mother, but Sonia somehow thought that was unlikely – she enjoyed the trappings of affluence too much to allow motherhood to intrude, and would soon be putting her energies into the plans Benjamin had for the Hall.

"Not the lilac, after all, Victoria" she commanded "it makes my skin look sallow. I will wear the dark blue dress - and find that pink pashmina dear Benjamin bought me last year."

She lay on the bed for precisely seven minutes, eyes closed, while the garments were found, then opening them, found she was slightly dizzy. Shaking her head slightly, she sat up carefully and decided to ask for assistance from Victoria, rather than dismissing her to prepare herself. Swiftly recovering, and having changed her dress, Sonia tried several pairs of heavy diamond earrings for effect before she decided on wearing the daintiest, to complement the silver thread embroidery on the fine cashmere.

"We used to call them stoles fifty years ago" she mused, sitting at the dressing table, while Victoria was busy with tail comb and spray. "Dances were known as 'hops', there were no such things as teenagers, and gentlemen accepted 'no' for an answer."

"It sounds dull to me" Victoria commented.

"You knew where you stood;" snapped Sonia acidly. "We had backbone, and standards. Something I want *you* to develop with regard to Benjamin's projects. The Hall has always been associated with quality. We may be new money compared with some of the families around here, but we certainly know how to conduct ourselves."

Even on this day, Sonia could not resist seizing an opportunity for training, Victoria thought, sullenly. It made her shudder and wonder if she was, after all, in the right place. Coming from an unremarkable local professional family, but determined to improve herself, her social ambition had apparently resurrected memories of the young Sonia, and this mirror image had formed an instant recognition when they first met. Sonia had seen in Benjamin's choice a worthy successor to her role as Lady of the Hall, and had set out to train Victoria to be her equal as a hostess, in preparation for Benjamin's business plans.

But could anyone be as ruthless at the core of her being, yet with that deceptively charming exterior, as Sonia had been, her daughter-in-law wondered. According to Ben, even Sir Geoffrey's final illness had never prompted a softer part of his wife, although she managed to retain a façade of caring in the presence of his private nurse. Victoria wielded the comb with a momentary lack of concentration.

"Don't pull, girl" Sonia snapped "now hold the mirror so that I may see the back properly. I thought so – do that part again, you've made it unbalanced."

Victoria sighed, straightened her back momentarily then bent to her task again, but at last completed Sonia's coiffure to her liking.

"There you are. Do you wish me to come downstairs with you?"

"Of course not. You may inform Benjamin that I am ready and we will make our appearance at three precisely. As it is two forty-five now, that leaves you time enough to get yourself prepared."

The young woman took heed of the note of dismissal in her mother-in-law's voice. She walked heavily along the corridors to the rooms she shared with Benjamin, and the adjoining dressing room that had been converted to make a nursery. Using the house phone, answered by a busy Annie, she announced that Lady Sonia was expecting her son in her room, then sank on the bed for one glorious moment of relaxation. Thank goodness there was only a month or so to endure this awful undignified physical state, where she felt like nothing on earth, where her moods were uncontrollable, and where the last person she wanted to see was her husband.

"Please God, let it be a boy, then I won't have to go through all this again" she prayed for the thousandth time. No time for dwelling on that now, though – no time for anything but a quick change of dress and refreshing her makeup. Reluctantly, with ill-grace and a supreme effort she rose and went to the bathroom.

Barbara was greeting and surreptitiously supervising the guests as they started to arrive at the Hall for about two forty-five, as instructed. Over thirty had received their invitations some weeks past, with very mixed reactions, as they realised that their own family traditions would have to be totally disrupted to accommodate Sonia's schedule. Husbands had grumbled, grandchildren had been puzzled and resentful, but it made no difference - husbands and wives concocted various excuses to justify the expected response and rearranged their own plans to suit the obligatory attendance; to step out of line would have social consequences that would affect lives for their foreseeable future.

"Like a command performance" was the least offensive comment expressed by many of those 'privileged' to be on the list. Selected W.I. members, fellow members of the charity committees chaired by Sonia for many years, the Vicar and his wife, head teachers of schools, representatives of the village clubs and societies which, if Sonia never actually graced them with her attendance, welcomed (at least in theory) the approval her invitation bestowed.

Neighbours were represented by a retired Colonel, and business connections by erstwhile 'captains of industry' with their wives. The guests stood around or sat in the drawing room, talking in low tones, clustered in small groups by the fireplace, by the grand piano, by the tall spruce tree firmly braced in a large tub and festooned with all its decorations. An air of tension mingled with the boredom, but most managed to conceal their resentment.

Barbara had let it be known that Sonia would appear at three o'clock precisely, and as the clock ticked on the last arrivals came breathlessly into the hallway.

"Barbara! How well you look!" Richard had a soft spot for his mother-in-law's best friend, and gave her an affectionate hug. "Say hello to Auntie Barbara, children."

They happily obliged, showing the small toys they had smuggled in their coat pockets, knowing she would join in their conspiracy. Jacqui gave her an affectionate hug and a whispered

"We'll have a chat later if we can manage it."

But with time ticking away there needed to be a hasty disposal of coats and gloves, then the family joined the other guests in the drawing room, shaking hands with a few, before Barbara stepped in, with a finger to her lips.

→4←

THE SUBDUED CHATTER DIED AS all the guests turned to look through the doorway. Sonia, with studied effect, came slowly and elegantly, down the curved staircase, one hand resting lightly on the balustrade, the other tucked warmly into the crook of Benjamin's arm. Following at a discreet distance was Victoria Jane. For a fleeting moment at the bottom of the stairway, as her mother paused, Jacqueline thought she looked quite fragile – but it *was* only an impression, and it *could* be a trick of the light ...

As Sonia entered the drawing room a spontaneous chorus of "Happy birthday to you" started from the corner where the choirmaster (representing the choir) sat at the piano and his wife (representing the Mothers' Union) stood by his side. Tension eased as the tune was taken up, fell apart raggedly at the line "happy birthday dear ..." with a mix of "Sonia, Lady Woolston, Granny, Mummy or Mother" depending on the connection of the singers, then a rousing last line of relief when all joined in with
"... Happy Birthday to *you* ..."
Sonia acknowledged the ripple of applause, sank into a large chair with a table at the side, and was soon busy with the procession of gift-bearers led by her grandchildren. The brave few who had brought nothing but themselves were glad to see the distraction of the trays of sherry brought round by Annie and Lisa, then replaced by further trays of champagne. Doris appeared, wheeling a dumb waiter with the magnificently iced and decorated cake, encrusted with yellow sugar roses and ribbons. This was the signal for Benjamin to clear his throat and tap a pen on his glass for attention, as he prepared to make a speech.

"Welcome to each and every one of you" he began in a pompous tone. "As you know, my mother has today reached her three score years and ten, and it is fitting that so many of her friends have been drawn together to celebrate the event. It was, I am sure, no accident that her birth coincided with another great birthday …"

The Vicar drew in a sharp breath, but Benjamin continued, oblivious to any potential offence.

"… and to commemorate her own significant day, a donation will be made to the village church in order to provide a new set of vestments, which will match the altar cloth she donated at the time of my father's death."

The Vicar looked startled, then pleased.

"… this gesture is so typical of my mother. Her generosity over the years has become well-known throughout the county and beyond. Every time anyone enters our church or attends a service they will be reminded of this."

Sonia allowed herself to pat her son's hand, and smiled up at him – an indulgent, self-satisfied smile that no-one could fail to notice.

"The connections with the world of business forged by my parents, have been passed on to me and will be maintained at every opportunity. I am glad to see them well represented here today."

This drew a nod of acknowledgement from the three prevailed upon to attend by their socially climbing wives, who simpered and preened in their finery.

"Finally, I had rather hoped that my wife would have already chosen to present us with an impeccably timed contribution to the next generation …"

Vicky refused to meet her husband's eyes and looked away from the glances of a less than tactful few, all strangers to her. None of her own friends had been invited, nor had that even been suggested, yet she would have given anything to have had someone present who was not family, someone who remembered her as she used to be, just for reassurance and an understanding glance.

"… but it was only a fleeting thought. How could this day be shared with any other – it belongs solely and indisputably to my mother and no one else, so I ask you to rise and toast the grandest woman in the county – Sonia, Lady Woolston."

Glasses were raised, and Sonia rose to formally make the first cut into the cake before it was taken away to the dining room. Chatter resumed, Sonia held court, and soon people were drifting into the dining room to make inroads on the food. The delicious savouries, prepared so lovingly by Doris and Lisa proved too tempting to ignore and disappeared surprisingly rapidly, given that many local guests had already consumed their Christmas lunches.

Small bite-sized sandwiches, tiny quiche tartlets and cream cheese roulades could not be resisted, and settled surprisingly well on to full stomachs, when accompanied by sherry, champagne and wine.

Vicky was glad of a chance to sit down after the toast. Jacqueline noticed this and went to her side.

"Anything you'd like to drink? A glass of water?"

Her offer was accepted gratefully. These days neither sherry nor champagne was palatable, and her obligatory glass sat untouched on a nearby table.

"I'm not prying, but if you're finding anything too difficult these days and I can help, do let me know. The last few weeks always seems to be such an endless stage."

Vicky managed a wan smile at her sister-in-law, then pulled herself together with an effort.

"Oh, but I *am* coping. Your mother is such a wonderful inspiration with her 'show must go on' approach, so I'm doing the same. I'm sure I will soon recover, and of course there will be the Nanny to help."

Jacqui remembered her own optimism as she had awaited the birth of Tim, trying to retain a 'normal' life for the benefit of her first husband, the wayward rock star who demanded his wife's total attention - when he remembered to come home. Ben was as likely as Zak had been to be intolerant of disruption, but now was certainly not the time to enlighten his wife. She returned with the water.

"Don't forget, I'm only a phone call away."

Her sister-in-law nodded.

Ella trotted over, her hands extended to show her mother how much chocolate had melted before it reached her mouth.

"Nonny gave it to me" she announced proudly "and Timmy's is even worser."

"Worse" her mother automatically corrected. " Come along – we need to wash this off. Timmy? Timmy – come with us … Do excuse us, Vicky."

Watching the little group steering through the guests, Victoria wondered again if she herself was really in the right place, with the right people, in the right life. She felt a shiver of something that felt like foreboding, and wished that she could disappear for a rest. The baby felt so heavy in her womb and everything took so much effort – another month of this was a huge mountain to climb.

She noticed that some early leavers were making their way to Sonia's chair to say farewell and congratulate her, having done their duty. Hopefully the rest would not take too long. One blessing of insisting on this day was that most people wanted to return to their own homes as soon as they decently could, and an hour was sufficient for most to feel they had done their duty, delivered their good wishes and have seen and been seen by the ones who noticed these finer points of etiquette. No sooner had the first bold few said their farewells than the majority took the opportunity to ask for their outer garments, and soon Annie and Lisa were dispensing coats and wraps, and ensuring no-one left anything behind.

"Victoria!"

Ben's voice came nearer. Aware he was under Sonia's watchful gaze, he bent to murmur discreetly in his wife's ear.

"Yes … yes. No, I'll be fine" she assured him. Moving as swiftly as she could she went across to Sonia and helped her mother-in-law to her feet. Sonia looked pale under her make-up and her eyes were dull, but she shrugged off any assistance once she was standing.

"I will rest for a while. Benjamin – attend to the remainder of our guests, Barbara will help you. Victoria - come upstairs with me and I will be down for dinner as usual."

The journey upstairs was slow, with many pauses for breath, but Sonia refused to allow Victoria to call Annie for help, or even Barbara. On reaching her room, she swayed and nearly lost her balance, but her daughter-in-law managed to steady her and help her to the bed, where she sank back on the pillows. Removing her shoes, Victoria made Sonia comfortable under the coverlet and noticed that a little colour was coming back into her cheeks.

Victoria was never very comfortable with other people's illnesses, and the thought of the indestructible Sonia succumbing to anything serious was unthinkable, so her bedside manner consisted of vaguely patting the bony hand lying on top of the counterpane and awaiting further instructions. None was forthcoming, so when Sonia's eyes closed and her breathing settled, she moved away from the bed and slipped out of the room. Her own chilliness had returned after the exertion of climbing the stairs with Sonia, and she walked through the corridors to her own room to collect a wrap for herself.

The guests had almost dispersed. Annie and Lisa had closed the dining room door and were starting to clear the debris of the elegant buffet. Jacqui was getting the children into their coats and Richard was shaking Ben's hand, formally thanking him for his hospitality.

Barbara longed for a cigarette. Once the little family was out of the way, she thought … these days one had to be so careful not to offend, particularly with Richard being a doctor. In any case, she was very fond of Jacqui and the way she had survived the unfair bias of her upbringing. It was a puzzle to her, close friend though she was, that no real reason had ever come to light for Sonia's blatant favouritism of Ben and overt resentment of his twin sister.

"I'll run upstairs and say goodbye on behalf of all of us" Jacqui said to her family, "get in the car and I'll be with you in just a minute."

A soft tap at her mother's half open door brought no response, so she pushed it open and walked in to leave a gentle kiss. Leaning over the still figure she immediately sensed that something was not right – not right at all. No faint breath against her cheek. Jacqui reached for her mother's hand, tried to locate the pulse spot on her wrist, then felt the side of Sonia's neck.

Victoria - where was Victoria?

Grabbing the house phone she waited an age, it seemed. Benjamin answered, irritated, then was stunned into silence.

"Ben, get Richard – I think mother's … quickly … *quickly* … and *please* come up here."

⇝5⇜

"YOU TOTALLY STUPID GIRL! I *knew* I should never have let an idiot like you get your hands on him ..... what sort of daughter-in-law are you ...... can't you see I'm not well ...... what *am* I doing up *here*? ...... you had no right to leave me ......"

Sonia's thoughts had screamed inside her head as she found herself gently floating up to the ceiling, moving in a soundless vacuum she couldn't explain. Her limbs were without sensation – or appeared to be, as the ceiling was there but she had no feeling of bumping against it. Now, looking down, she saw herself lying peacefully on the bed, apparently asleep. Why was she *here* when she should be *there*?

"Get me out of here! Benjamin, Barbara – help me to come back!"

The phone – that would solve it. One ring and her beloved Benjamin would come running and take care of everything. She looked down again and tried to reach out ... but nothing in her arm responded. It must be part of whatever she was dreaming ... if she shut her eyes then it would all be back to normal. But even her eyelids would not obey. She felt trapped. There was no pain, not even an ache, just this ridiculous situation where she was pinned up against the ceiling, unable to speak or move, and with nobody there to see her predicament.

There was a tap at the bedroom door. It opened - how *dare* anyone enter without receiving her permission ... Jacqueline moved quickly to the bed and bent down.

Sonia, at first puzzled, then horrified, watched her daughter's reaction – the way she held her mother's wrist, the way she felt for a pulse in her neck, the swiftness with which she seized the bedside telephone - and the urgency

31

with which she then ran to the door and shouted for Richard to come quickly. Benjamin came rushing into the room first, then Richard, followed by Annie at a discreet distance, and Barbara, of course – all showing great concern.

Benjamin falling to his knees at the side of the bed, trying to get warmth into his mother's hand. Richard did what Jacqueline had done – felt her pulse, raised her eyelids, then shook his head gravely at the waiting family.

Having at first thought she looked asleep, now her body looked lifeless, thought Sonia, yet it could not really be so – all that was needed was for it to be joined up again with the real Sonia who was *here*, waiting, floating above. She kept trying to pull against the force that held her apart from the empty shape on the bed, but nothing in this new situation would respond. Helpless, she continued to watch the scene below.

Her own doctor appeared, recalled from his early escape from the party. He used his stethoscope, checked pulses and, looking very serious, spoke to all of the assembled family in the room. Sonia couldn't hear what he said, but Jacqueline turned to her husband and wept. Richard put his arm around her, comfortingly. Ben, looking stony faced, gazed long and hard at his mother's body, then suddenly clenched his fists and turned swiftly away and out of the room, shrugging aside Victoria's attempt to hold his hand, snapping something under his breath at her, so that she visibly cringed. Barbara moved over to Sonia and patted her hand helplessly, tears streaming down her face.

The looks on their faces were the looks that people wore in old movies, Sonia thought. It was all too bizarre, when here she was, desperately wanting them to look up so they would see her and bring her back down.

Why were there no attempts at resuscitation? What was the doctor thinking of?

There should be ambulances and people rushing around with equipment and shocking her body back into life, instead of this attitude of acceptance. Again and again she tried to make herself heard, but it was no use, obviously they could not hear anything. Eventually she was forced to accept that she was wasting her time and became resigned to a situation that she only half understood – not wanting to acknowledge the full implication of something she had never encountered in her beliefs about the process of death.

Was she destined to spend eternity in this ridiculous space? Hovering around in her room for evermore? Eventually the fuss beneath her calmed down. One by one the family left the room until only Jacqueline remained.

Her daughter's face was full of love as she tenderly stroked Sonia's cheek and tucked a stray wisp of hair into place.

"Oh Mummy, I *do* wish you peace at last. Please forgive me if I haven't been the daughter you hoped for. I hope you will be together with Daddy, and happy again."

A discreet tap at the door, and Annie entered with two men in suits whom Sonia had never seen before.

Sonia became aware that she, of all people, was powerless to do anything. It was an alarming thought that she had no control over anything for the first time for many decades. Then just as the implication dawned of the undertaker's men coming into her room, the ceiling apparently dissolved so that she could move through and she passed into a void.

A small part of her still wanted to return to her bedroom, which was now growing smaller and more distant. Sonia tried to reach back, to clutch the edges of the dissolving ceiling, but there was nothing to feel, nothing to hold, no sensation in her fingers.

All the walls had evaporated and she could see Ben pacing along the corridors outside his room. Jacqueline and Richard were moving down the stairs, then to the kitchen where Doris was fussing around, trying to distract the children from asking too many questions. Now even the Hall, with everything and everyone in it seemed to be getting even smaller, as if she were looking at the scenes through the wrong end of a telescope.

Everything became a velvety blackness that should have been threatening, yet somehow was not. It was warm and soft, and immensely soothing – a feeling as if she was being drawn into the softest feather down – no pain, no anxiety, nothing but peace. A pinpoint of light in the distance was drawing her towards it, as if it was a powerful magnet - yet lights did not magnetise, so why did it feel that way? The light continued to exert its influence. Powerless to resist, she felt an increase of speed as the light grew larger and brighter, then she was being rushed along through an upward vortex of brilliance towards … towards … where?

There was an impression of moving through warmth and exquisite perfumes, sounds like no others she had ever heard, colours like no others she had ever seen – all fleetingly, tantalisingly passing before she had time to dwell on them. Vast oceans passed beneath her and mountain ranges appeared in grey mistiness, too far below to endanger her progress. It seemed endless and very strange. She was aware of robed figures appearing and melting away as soon as she had focussed on them. Strange buildings appeared in the landscape and were soon lost to sight. She had no indication of how her flight was taking place – it just seemed to happen. It *must* be a dream.

Then at last all movement stopped.

Sonia found that she was standing in a meadow of luxuriant grass, with drifts of many exquisite flowers appearing at her feet in the most incredibly beautiful colours that she could never recall having seen anywhere before. A fringe of trees lined the edge of the meadow, which extended as far as she could see, gently undulating and with a warm perfumed waft of a breeze that hardly stirred the grass, yet which set the intense colours of the flowers shimmering and dancing before her eyes. But it was the lake that captured her attention. It was like no other lake she had seen – fathomless, dark and mysterious, reaching from a distant point somewhere unknown past the horizon. A boat appeared from a misty distance, moving silently without any apparent method of propulsion and slowly, with dignity, coming to rest at the bank a short distance away.

A figure appeared at the helm of the boat and motioned to her to step in. Sonia hesitated and looked around, wondering if she had a choice. She wanted to stay with the flowers in the meadow and reflect on what had happened. But even as the thought passed through her mind it detached itself and floated away like a wisp of gossamer. She had no choice.

Her arm was steadied as she stepped into the boat and she lay down on soft seating, closed her eyes and let matters take their own course. She had no resistance left, and felt as if she could sleep forever. Time seemed to have ceased, and in any case there was no way of measuring it. It could have been hours or minutes - or even days, she thought, as the gentle rhythmic sound of muffled oars lulled her into another sleep. Rousing later, she thought she saw another bank where there were some indistinct figures who melted away when they saw her - all except one, who helped fasten the craft to a tree at the bank, and offered a hand to assist her out of the boat, before escorting her along a path.

This countryside was different – another meadow, certainly, but the grass was as closely cut as the finest English lawn. No wild flowers here, but at intervals there were drifts of plants and flowers she recognised – large hostas, sweet-smelling freesias and lilies, all somehow emerging from the edge of the trees in a way they would never have been landscaped on Earth, and again with the intense colours that almost dazzled her. The pathway took a turn at the end of a copse, and looking ahead, it led to a marble house built in the classical style. They walked up a flight of shallow steps onto a balustraded area that extended around the building, then through a space between two pillars that led inside.

The interior was light and cool, and the whole atmosphere was very similar to ancient Grecian paintings. A gathering was in progress in a vast hall that lay behind the façade, and gentle conversation could be heard, as well as music. Sonia momentarily expected it to be a welcoming party, but she was not allowed to stop. Her escort whisked her through corridors, then in through a doorway to an anteroom where there was a couch, and motioned her to sit.

She tried to see who her guide had been, but he was wearing a hooded garment that shaded his face, and melted away before she could focus properly. Sitting on the couch, she tried to recall all the events of the day, tried to connect things one to another and make sense of it all, but it became too much, so she gave up, wondering what would happen next.

Waking later, Sonia found she was lying in her own bed. She tentatively stretched her arms then her legs, and found to her amazement that she could move more freely than she ever remembered doing since she was a young woman. Sitting up, she looked around cautiously. The room was the same, with the curtains half-drawn together. All her usual possessions were lying on the dressing table – the jewel case, the silver-backed comb and brushes, the photographs. Relieved that it had all been a dream - or a nightmare - Sonia reached for the telephone to summon Annie to attend to her. But there was no phone. She looked around with more attention to detail.

All looked very normal ... and yet ... and yet ... there was definitely something different. Glancing upwards, she noticed with surprise that the walls appeared to have no limits - they just disappeared into a vague golden mistiness of gossamer threads. A trick of the light, she assumed, suddenly feeling very tired again, so she sank back into her pillows and allowed drowsiness to overtake her once more. But when she woke later and optimistically looked around what seemed so familiar, it was the same appearance turning out to be the same delusion.

Where *was* everyone?

A thought struck her that was so odd she dismissed it instantly, but then it came back again – was it possible that this was *death*? But no, it couldn't be – where were the trumpet fanfares? Where was the welcoming party of all those who had been waiting to see her? Where were all the Heavenly hosts, the choirs of Angels, the Cherubim and Seraphim?

It was a pleasant enough setting, of course it was – but could this be what was meant by the house of many mansions? Surely not. Yet here she was, in some sort of a replica of her room at the Hall and with no-one to greet her – not at all what she had been led to expect by the Church's teachings.

Cautiously she tested the floor with one foot then both, then found she was able to rise swiftly and naturally - no need for the light cane she had been using lately – and moved across the room to the door, intending to summon Annie or Benjamin – anyone. But it had no handle or any visible means of opening it from inside and showed no sign of yielding to the firmest push. Moving across to the window she could see that the view outside was certainly not the view she was used to seeing from the Hall.

This was pleasant enough – gardens, countryside and even a glimpse of some far-off expanse of water, although whether it was lake or sea was impossible to tell, and in the far distance beyond a hint of mountain ranges. But - no gentle English hills rising into the distance, no village roofs visible a mile away, no lodge by the gateway …

… it most definitely was not Surrey … not England … not home.

→6←

FRANTIC HASTE GAVE WAY TO a whole range of mixed reactions at the Hall. Richard had waited in the room until Sonia's own Doctor returned, hastily summoned back from his fireside where he was just starting to relax from attending the birthday party. He examined Sonia's body, confirmed Richard's report, made notes, then went to discuss matters with Ben.

Jacqui had retrieved the children from the car and was waiting with them in the drawing room that had so recently been full of people paying tribute to their hostess. It was unbelievable. The children, sensing that they ought to be solemn, actually were, but were very pleased when Doris came to ask if they would like to have biscuits and a drink with her and Lisa in the kitchen. Jacqui gave her a grateful smile.

→←

"A massive stroke" Dr Hartley pronounced, when he came down the stairs. "She wouldn't have known much about it, really – who was the last one to see her?"

"Vicky took Mummy up to her room" Benjamin said as he followed behind. "Where is she? I haven't seen her – do *you* need to see her, doctor?"

"I should, for the paperwork. And in any case I should check up on *her* – don't want her going into shock at this stage, do we?"

"I'll go and find her first – I just want a word ..."

Ben went back upstairs, his tumbling thoughts in free-fall. She couldn't. Not Mummy. She wasn't ready to die – *he* wasn't ready to let her go. There was so much she had to do before she handed everything over to him. She couldn't leave like this, not with the baby about to arrive, and how would he cope with Vicky? Vicky – why oh why did it have to be *her*? What an *idiot* she was. She'd be nothing without Sonia to steer her, advise her and make sure she maintained the standards ... by the time he reached their room he was even more full of frustration and anger.

Vicky waited, sitting hunched wretchedly on the bed, recognising the footsteps along the corridor to be Ben's impatient rush. She was not, however, expecting the door to be slammed and to be the subject of his towering rage.

"*My* mother – the one woman who understood me" he fumed, "and you couldn't even be trusted to take care of her for five minutes. You must have *known* she was ill. You couldn't even be bothered to lift the phone. You think you're going to run this place? – you're not fit to take over a market stall."

Even with the door shut, he could be heard from the head of the stairs. The tirade went on and on, with his wife flinching at every phrase, unable to speak, and certainly unable to defend herself. She cringed at every word, hoping he would stop if he saw how much he was hurting her, but her reactions only served to increase his fury.

"Don't sit there snivelling, you wretched girl. If it wasn't for the child you'd have been booted out long ago, as well you know. You've made things ten times worse for everyone ..."

A knock at the door while he paused for breath made him come to his senses.

"Ben!" it was his sister, who was truly appalled by what she heard as she came up the stairs followed by the somewhat embarrassed family doctor.

"Ben – you need to come and deal with things downstairs. I'll join you when Dr Hartley's seen Vicky."

The doctor tactfully avoided any reference to what he had overheard and dealt with the necessary questions as briefly and sympathetically as possible, asking Victoria if she had noticed any unusual signs that Sonia was not feeling well, but she was too upset to say much. He offered to send her to hospital, but she adamantly refused, insisting she was just tired, even though it would have been tempting to take that line of escape – but no, it wouldn't be worth the risk of adding further fuel to Ben's rage. The Doctor reluctantly gave her a sedative and persuaded her to lie down.

"I would have preferred her to go to the hospital to keep an eye on the situation, but I'll call back in the morning" Dr Hartley said to Jacqueline who had waited outside the room. He watched Victoria sink into an exhausted sleep.

"If you're going now, could you tell Richard I'll be down in a moment and could you find out if Barbara can take over?" Jacqueline asked him. "We must take the children home, I want to reassure them and help them get used to things."

She went back to Sonia's room and knelt at the side of the bed, stroking her mother's hair, holding her hand, tears falling as she whispered a few words to the still figure. Getting to her feet when Barbara joined her, they both stood quietly holding hands for a few moments.

"Can you stay with Mummy until they come to ... to ...?" she choked back more tears. "I really must get the children back home."

"Of course I will. They need you. I'll look after things here, and keep an eye on everyone."

They embraced, and Jacqueline took one last look.

The journey back home was such a contrast from the excited anticipation a few hours earlier. Their mother sat in the back of the car with the children, reassuring them with warm cuddles, but there was no hiding the fact that Richard and Jacqui were subdued.

"Will it mean we won't ever see Nonny again?" Ella asked.

"She'll come and see you when you're asleep. You'll dream about her, then you'll know she's been."

Tim felt suddenly grown up.

"Will she be with Gramps?" He could just about remember his grandfather's kindly ways and the smell of his tweed gardening jacket. Geoffrey had died just before Tim was two, but there had been a strong bond between them and a special photograph was always in his room at home – Gramps bending down to hold his hand as they walked in the garden at the Hall, not many weeks before the heart attack claimed him.

"They'll be together now, and probably walking in a garden, smelling the flowers" Jacqui responded, picking up his thoughts. She gave him a gentle hug. The death of his grandfather, then later his stepfather, who was also abruptly taken from his life just as he was really getting to know him - too many changes and losses for a child his age, Jacqueline feared, but she had done everything she could to help him accept and understand. It was a difficult period for them both, but her pregnancy had helped to heal the sadness that Anthony would never even see his child.

The arrival of his little half sister had been a blessing in many ways, and although Jacqueline had little support from her mother she attributed that to her mother's continuing grief, hidden behind a mask of seeming indifference. Staying with her policy of remaining in touch, her patience eventually produced results, and Ella, once introduced to her Grandmother, proved to be a child that Sonia unexpectedly warmed to (providing of course that she did not have to encounter her too frequently), and the old rift at last had showed signs of beginning to heal.

Jacqui hoped that none of Ben's rage had been audible downstairs. She was a great believer in adult conversations, particularly emotional ones, remaining just that – for adult ears only. The children dozed, snuggled up against her, one each side, in the warm car, and the quiet minutes gave her time to ponder that scene. Her brother could be volatile, she knew, but even making allowances for the shock he too must have been feeling, there was no need to round on his wife in that way. It did not bode well for that relationship, she mused – but perhaps things would improve once the baby arrived and they could settle down as a family.

Arriving home, the holly wreath on the front door of the neat house in the suburbs looked welcoming. Richard helped Jacqui carry the children out of the car and into the warmth of their sitting room. Putting them at each end of the long sofa, she covered them with the bright crocheted blankets she kept downstairs for times when security and comfort were what an upset child needed. She and Richard sat drinking hot chocolate, talking in low tones and making sure the children were undisturbed, not wanting them to wake on their own. Richard held her hand.

"You were a brick" he said tenderly "thank you for looking after Vicky like that."

"I hope she'll be alright. The doctor seemed to think that a few hour's sleep would help, but Ben's attitude worried me more than I can say. I'm just glad I was there."

"Shock can have some really strange effects, Jacqui – fortunately he'll be kept busy with the funeral arrangements, and it will all blow over, I'm sure. All we can do is wait to hear from him about what he needs us to do. Phone by all means – but not tonight. Let's concentrate on the children and you."

The rest of that evening was occupied in looking after the children's needs and making things as normal as possible. Later that night, emotionally drained, Jacqui dreamed as she eventually slept fitfully. Her father was there, and walking with Anthony her second husband. They held out their hands to her, then moved away. After that, the second part of her night's sleep was easier.

Barbara had taken over from Jacqueline's vigil, but once she was satisfied that Victoria was truly asleep, had crept downstairs again. Vicky had slept for a couple of hours, then woke alone, with a stabbing pain in her head, and a dull ache in her back shooting down her legs. The awful scene with Ben came flooding back into her consciousness as she tried to ease herself into a better position, then the ache became more insistent.

"No, please no …" she muttered through another wave of pain "I'm not ready, I can't …"

She waited a while longer, terrified of what she instinctively knew was about to happen, and her own unpreparedness. Carefully walking slowly down the stairs she could hear Ben and Barbara in the Library - thankfully realising he was not on his own gave her the courage to face him. Pushing the door open she saw them sitting either side of the fireplace, brandy glasses in hand, Barbara with the inevitable full ashtray on the table at her side. But thank goodness Barbara was there – it was another woman she needed at this moment.

"Oh God, it's that bloody wife of mine, the one who killed my mother."

Vicky's face crumpled with humiliation as she clutched the door handle, pain surging through her body.

"Barbara, I think I … I need … " she caught her breath and sank to the floor.

However much Barbara had to drink, she always seemed to be able to function when there was an emergency. The ambulance eventually arrived, but Ben refused to go to hospital with his wife who wept and screamed when he came near, so it was Barbara who accompanied her.

Three hours of confusion later, Victoria gave birth to a healthy girl. Barbara telephoned the Hall just before midnight to tell Ben the news. There was no answer, except from Annie who was sitting by the extension in the Lodge and who reassured her that he had safely gone to bed, not adding that he had staggered off with another bottle, even though she was sure Barbara would not have turned a hair at the news.

Barbara saw that Vicky was settled down for the night, made excuses to her and the hospital staff for Ben's non-appearance, ordered a taxi and returned to the Lodge, where Annie was waiting for more news.

It took another hour and several brandies to relay all the details. Barbara and Annie had become well acquainted over the years of Barbara visiting the Hall to assist Sonia; there was nothing to draw them into a close friendship – that would have been inappropriate in Sonia's eyes, who always had firm lines of demarcation drawn for her staff. Because Annie's position was more that of maid than companion, whenever Barbara visited she was expected to wait on her too, although Barbara was careful not to make her tasks too onerous.

Once the facts of the birth had been dealt with, the two women sat in the cosy front room of the gatehouse, reminiscing over good times and difficult ones. Annie confided that she felt it might be time to move on now that Sonia had died.

"I'm under no illusion about how things would be – even if Mr Benjamin said he wanted me to stay on, the new Mrs Woolston would feel that I was forever comparing her with her mother-in-law. I'm not intending to do it straight away, in the circumstances, but I won't hang on indefinitely. The next few days are going to seem very strange, though."

"It's not every day you have a death and a birth in one family. Come to think of it, it's not every day that someone becomes an orphan and a father within hours. I'd like to help, so I shall offer to stay on and assist Benjamin with practical things, give moral support, even though he may think he doesn't want that. We don't want him to go to pieces, but I do urge you to reconsider, Annie – things will be difficult enough for them."

"There's nothing now to keep me here. I only stayed because I promised Geoffrey …" Annie checked herself, but unspoken words hung thick in the air.

Barbara looked at her curiously. The familiarity was out of character and she sensed that Annie might have been about to add something that she could have regretted the next day, but they were both exhausted by the tensions of the day, to say nothing of the turn events had taken, and she let it pass.

"Come along then, time for bed or we'll be fit for nothing in the morning. We're going to need all our wits about us, dealing with birth, death and everything in between." Her brisker tone prevented the possible descent into shared confidences. Annie responded, albeit reluctantly – wishing, not for the first time, that she herself had someone close and trustworthy to talk with.

Barbara eventually dozed off to sleep in the spare bedroom at the Lodge that Annie had prepared for her while waiting for news from the hospital, rather than risk disturbing anyone at the Hall. She slept fitfully after hazily sifting through a jumble of thoughts. Benjamin could be dealt with in the morning, and by the sound of it, would not be in a fit state to do a great deal until the day was well under way. Thanks to the promptness of the funeral directors, Sonia was safely in their Chapel of Rest in Guildford. Official paperwork could not be dealt with until after the holiday period was over, which meant that the funeral arrangements would probably not be made for another week or so …

She slept soundly enough until Annie came through with coffee, then walked over to the Hall to have a shower and exchange the long maroon bead-encrusted dinner dress which had seen so many fraught situations in the last twenty four hours, for something more practical.

Benjamin had appeared, somewhat shamefaced, for a very late breakfast, and seeing Barbara's expression swiftly contacted George to take him to the hospital. Victoria sat in bed in the private ward feeling as miserable as she could ever remember. Her daughter lay in a crib, having been in the baby ward for the most part of the night. There had not been much chance of Victoria getting any sleep, though, the events of the past day kept running through her mind, and on top of that, the natural hormonal changes and emotions of giving birth were making her head spin.

She heard Benjamin's footsteps outside the door. It opened slowly and a huge bouquet of flowers appeared, waving slowly - it was Ben - hoping that Vicky would not remember they had been on display at the birthday party. Sheepishly emerging from behind the flowers was Ben's face, looking blotched and apprehensive. He moved over to the bed and bent to kiss his wife, with a waft of peppermint breath to disguise any trace of last night's brandy and the morning's 'hair of the dog'.

"Darling, I owe you the most abject apology – will you ever be able to forgive me? Where's our daughter? I need to see if she's as beautiful as you."

Vicky was disarmed, as indeed she wanted to be. At this stage of their marriage Ben's apologetic moods were to be responded to and treasured, with the upset never referred to again, giving time for both of them to forget the cause. They both spent a long time discussing their daughter, neither really wanting to broach the subject of Sonia's death.

But eventually, Vicky held Ben's hand and asked what had happened after she left. Ben stood up abruptly and walked to the window, not answering immediately, until, taking a deep breath, he tersely informed her that she would not have to answer any more questions from the doctor, the certificate had been signed, and he expected her to be well enough to be at his side for the funeral, which would take place after New Year.

Then, subject closed, he returned to the seat by the bed and dutifully gazed at his daughter again, only leaving when she woke and Victoria said she was going to feed her.

⇢7⇠

SONIA AWOKE, STILL SOMEWHAT DAZED. Looking around with a feeling of unease, she realised that what she vaguely remembered was indeed no dream after all. As before, it certainly appeared to be her room, but with no ceiling – just the walls rising into a mist. No familiar sounds of domesticity, no discreet tap at the door with Annie bringing her breakfast tray. She went over to the window and looked out, hoping against hope for the usual view across the Hall's familiar parkland, but again it was the different scene of an unknown landscape. What was she supposed to do? It was impossible to think that if indeed she *were* dead – she shuddered at the thought - that this could be her situation for evermore.

Then she recovered her old equilibrium and felt her normal reactions rise to the surface - in fact, it was *unpardonable* if that were so – at the very least she should have been given some sort of explanation – was there really nothing to do but wait? No, it was definitely *not* possible – it had been a nightmare and she was still in it – she had not woken at all. A feeling of irritation started to dominate, and the longer she waited, the stronger it grew. No telephone by her bed, the door still would not open, and there appeared to be no-one about within call.

It most definitely was not what she expected, and most certainly was not good enough. By the time there was a discreet cough behind her, she was more than ready to demand explanations in her usual authoritarian style.

A diminutive figure stood respectfully at a distance. He was no more than five feet tall, although as he had a slight stoop he could possibly have originally been taller, and he was definitely on the portly side. Thin wisps of pepper-and-salt hair were revealed as he took off a cloth hat of indeterminate design and stood holding it in gnarled hands. He was dressed in a charcoal grey robe that

45

was circled by a knotted cord and finished in an uneven hemline just above bare ankles, his feet in worn old leather sandals. Presumably some menial sort of monk, Sonia thought. He looked almost hesitant. She interpreted this as not being used to speaking to a lady.

This gave Sonia the upper hand - servant class without a doubt - but at least he was someone she could make use of ...

"And who might you be?" she snapped.

"I'm your Guide" he said, with a slight bow "and although we've hardly ever been in touch through your life, you'll soon come to realise that I've been with you at all times, just waiting for you to want me."

His voice had a lower class accent that Sonia realised, with a start, was reminiscent of the area where she had been born and raised; those cadences she had eliminated from her own speech, the vowels so different from the cultured ones she had worked so hard to acquire.

I *must* still be dreaming, Sonia thought – I'm probably running a fever, which would account for the muddled thinking and the visual distortions. She turned back to the bed, only to find that it had gone, replaced by her study at the Hall – again with the walls disappearing into the mist. Her desk was there, with notepaper and pens – looking as if she were about to start her usual morning's correspondence.

"You won't need your bed again because you won't need to rest," the strange man said. "You're here to learn and understand."

"I most certainly am not! Please put everything back in place, summon someone senior to help me, then be on your way. Whoever you are, you are not one of *my* employees, so kindly leave and you will hear no more of the matter."

"Ah – I thought so! You don't realise what has happened" he said, taking no notice of her instructions. "Now sit down and listen carefully - this sometimes comes as a shock when people are not prepared for the journey. I'm afraid there's no easy way of putting it, and I don't want to upset you – it's just that you had to come here so suddenly. This is the Afterlife and, like I said, I'm your Guide."

Sonia looked as she had never looked at any stage in her life - totally nonplussed. To have vague suspicions was one thing, but to have the confirmation of death thrust at her in this way destroyed all the hopes that the whole thing would turn out to be the nightmare she felt it to be.

"You are trying to tell me that I have *died*? But I am here in the Hall. I have only to call Annie and she will be here with the coffee and everything will be back to normal. It's Boxing Day, Barbara and I are expected at the Nelson's for lunch, then on to Jacqueline's for tea with the children. No, what you say is totally impossible. Now *go* - before I get *really* upset."

"But Sonia ..."

"How *dare* you be so familiar! On whose authority do you speak? Get out, get *out*! You do not look like any Guide and you certainly do not speak like one! Who are you supposed to be guiding and where? You come here to my room dressed in the oddest clothes that would disgrace even the gardener at the Hall, and you try to dictate what I shall do? Get *out* I say!"

He withdrew to a respectful distance, as the fury Sonia usually reserved for incompetent tradespeople was unleashed. It was just as he'd feared when he read the advance notice from Above that it was her time to be called – this one was going to take longer, and he would need all his powers of persuasion to get her even to the point of starting the work she had to do. There had been no opportunity to work with her during her Earth life, as she had made no contact with him. She had no real spiritual side – oh yes, he had seen her attending church regularly, but knew that it was for her own ambitions and not for her genuine spiritual development.

Sighing, and clasping his hands under his robe, he prayed as he faded away from the room.

> "Oh dear Lord, please help me. These sudden ones are always the worst (give me a nice contemplated suicide any day). Lord, I tried to be gentle but she's so arrogant. I'm going to leave her with the angels for a while until she's calmed down, then I'll return to try again. Amen."

Immediately, Sonia had the oddest feeling – as if her thoughts were being enfolded in soft downy wings. This soothed Sonia for a while, as did the realisation that she was once more on her own, but in spite of the comforting sensations, she still rationalised that she was dreaming and would wake up. But now there was undoubtedly a niggling doubt. What nonsense, she told herself, and having decided that indeed it *was* a dream, determined that she would take advantage of the opportunity and see if she could go outside for a breath of fresh air. Her thoughts had not stopped veering from one thing to another. Perhaps this would help.

Stepping through the French windows she found herself in the most delightful garden. Wandering among the herbaceous borders with all the flowers at their peak, it seemed to her gardener's eye too good to be true. Flowers changed as she approached, which was odd in itself – but flowers? On Boxing Day? These borders were June borders. Maybe they were in a large dome of some sort of perpetual climate, like the Eden project in Cornwall she had visited with Barbara last year. Yes, that was the only possible explanation, and condensation would explain this wretched mist everywhere, indoors and out, yet the light had an intense quality that she had never seen anywhere else on earth.

Sitting on a smooth wooden bench, trying to piece together her vague impressions of all that had happened, she could remember no pain – no, she mused, it had started with a bright light and warmth. Then there had been a feeling of travelling over mountains and rivers, coastlines laid out as if on a globe. All as if she were taking off in a plane in some way, but with no feeling of having to look through an aircraft's window. The light had become brighter and brighter until she felt that it and she were one, and she must have fallen asleep, only to wake and find that although there were certain similarities to her rooms at the Hall, there were also major differences that made it feel not quite genuine.

But the Afterlife? No, it *couldn't* be. That awful little man would have to find a way to prove it to her before she believed him. All her life she had understood and followed the Church's teaching, so of course she *knew* what lay ahead. It was precisely that understanding that had led her to be so significant a part of worship in the village, setting an example to all. It was one of the things that was so comfortable about village life – the division between churchgoers and those who did not get involved – one could conveniently forget the ones not seen on Sundays and simplify the village contacts, leaving room for other, more important things. In that traditional setting it was important to have a vicar who was also a traditionalist, and of course she used every influence she or her fellow churchgoers had to maintain that – the village would most certainly not respond to any of the more radical ideas that were around, and the merest whisper of the possibility of a woman being considered, for instance, had ensured that any number of significant strings had had to be pulled. Consequently, the current vicar was under no misapprehensions about his position and what he was expected to do. Moreover, any slight step out of line would earn him an imperious note from the Hall – Lady Sonia had many ways of organising even her spiritual life to her own taste. The thought that she might have to reconsider aspects of her belief was not something she was really prepared to contemplate.

The angels' wings persisted and eventually performed their task of soothing her, so that a slight curiosity ousted some of her resentment, and turned into resolve - if there were to be a challenge, then she would rise to it – she had never been afraid of meeting challenges head-on, from whatever quarter they came.

He was waiting when she returned, and motioned her to sit at her desk. Surprising herself, Sonia did so without protest.

"Have you had a nice walk?" he enquired solicitously. "You need to know that although we'll be working closely together it won't be without its rewards, and knowing you've been such a keen gardener I arranged for you to have the best place for your stay."

"For my stay? Does that imply that this is only a temporary arrangement? For heaven's sake, please tell me what exactly I am to expect."

"Dear *Lady* Sonia, if that's how you like to be addressed, I'm only too happy to explain, but please try to listen without interrupting me.

"As you now know, you're in the Afterlife – in other words, your soul has left its last body behind on Earth and you had a long journey to this place, which is called the Review Centre. It's where souls come to review their life, and their guide (that's me, of course) helps them to assess how many of their life's lessons they have learned. Later, …"

But he was not allowed to pause for breath before Sonia rose to her feet, her old attitude to the fore, her voice icy.

"I have never in my life heard such arrant nonsense. How dare you talk to me in this way when I know full well what the system is! None of this sentimental New Age rubbish, if you please –I had enough of that from my daughter. I have attended church for many, *many* years and I know that without doubt what is waiting for me is a place in one of the Lord's many mansions and, as is befitting one who has done so many good deeds, I shall be sat on the right hand of God Almighty Himself. If you continue to harass me in this way I shall not be answerable for the consequences."

She stalked out of the doorway and returned to the garden. This time her guide briefly cast his eyes upwards, muttered, and after apparently receiving approval, plucked up courage and followed her, his sandals flapping slightly in his haste.

"Dear Lady Sonia, please hear me out. This is all very new to you, but it's what you *have* to do and I can't change things. Look, let me show you something - it will help you understand." So saying, he stepped nearer and took her hand.

Before Sonia could open her mouth to protest she felt enveloped in the soft downy feeling once more and an impression of immense speed, but then it was all over very quickly and she suddenly found herself breathless and dizzy, in the corner of the kitchen at the Hall.

Annie and Doris sat at the large table in the kitchen. It was piled high, as every available space was - occupied with glasses and china, overflowing ashtrays and remnants of the feast that Doris had prepared for her deceased employer's birthday party. Lighting another cigarette – absolutely forbidden behaviour in any part of the Hall at all times among servants - she kicked off her shoes and drew up a chair to put her feet on.

Sonia stepped forward to remonstrate, and to find out why clearing away after the party had not been finished, but they totally ignored her, except for Annie giving a little shiver. Horrified, Sonia realised they could not see her. However awful the thought that she was indeed dead, it must be so. The conversation confirmed it without doubt.

"Have they all gone, then, Annie?"

"Just old Mrs Nelson waiting for George and the car because she's had several sherries too many. I found her quietly snoring her head off in the corner of the drawing room, so I organised Lisa into looking after her. He should be here in a minute and they can all go home."

"With Mr Benjamin sulking through several bottles in the Library and now Miss Victoria in hospital with Miss Barbara, we'll be safe for a good few hours yet. What a way to end a party – a death *and* a birth!"

Doris felt her mood suddenly lift, and continued.

"Look, I've been thinking, Annie – this *could* be the perfect timing. We've agreed that neither of us could ever face working for Miss Victoria and that's going to happen sooner than we thought, in the circumstances. Get Madam's funeral over and done with, the Nanny installed and I'll hand in my notice. You might be needed for a while longer, I suppose ...?"

"I may be *expected* to stay on, but there's no reason why I *should*. Sonia's death has released me from all obligations, I'm ready to start living my own life and I certainly intend doing just that, and as far away as possible. The only one I shall miss is Jacqueline – and the children, of course - but I want to have a retirement I can enjoy, and the sooner the better."

The two women carried on chatting about possible dates for the funeral, and what might be needed for the arrangements for guests, but it was all too much for Sonia. She had heard more than enough, and aghast, turned to find the little man at her side.

"Have you seen enough for now?" he enquired. She nodded, bewildered.

The speed, the sensations happened again, and they were returned to their previous setting in the garden.

→8←

"LET ME EXPLAIN MORE ..."

Sonia reluctantly decided to hear what he had to say. There *had* to be some explanation for the scene she had just witnessed. It had been torture to hear and see two people she had trusted for so many years, behaving as they did – only hours after the party had finished.

"First tell me who you are" she said firmly. "You do not seem to be a person of any significance, but you appear to have certain skills and I may as well use your name."

"My titles wouldn't mean anything to you, and my actual name is of no importance, but you may call me Master, and I'm your teacher in the Afterlife."

Sonia thought she had no reserves of energy left, but at this she raged yet again.

"*Master*? No-one is *my* 'master'. What a preposterous idea! You look like that down and out person Geoffrey once brought back with him from some Eastern trip - *he* turned out to be a real help in the garden, which was his saving grace – but I have yet to discover yours! Now get your explanation over and done with so that I may have some peace. And I shall name you Fu – *Mister* Fu – after the gardener!"

There was a small sigh – perhaps of resignation.

"Whatever you say, Lady Sonia - *whatever* you say on the matter, if it helps you do what you're here for. Now I think you've just had proof that you're indeed finished with that Earthly life you occupied for exactly seventy years. I'm sorry it had to be such a shock, but sometimes swift pain is better than prolonged discomfort. While you're going through these first stages of adjusting to your situation, you might find it helpful to know you're allowed to have as many visits to your old life as you wish. You only have to say and I'll come with you - the sooner we can get to the point of you *really* starting work, the better. It quite often helps people get another perspective on what we're doing. But be warned – you may not experience what you hope to find."

"I have nothing to fear from returning. I have led a blameless life, as you will hear. What we saw and heard Annie and Doris talking about was a natural shock reaction to the loss of their dear employer. They will soon come to their senses." Sonia snapped.

The little man looked at her quizzically, decided not to pursue the matter and resumed.

"Now - the work I mentioned. We need to look at the effect you had on other people's lives – good and bad. Then there are the lessons ..."

Sonia's mouth opened, but he hastily continued.

"… you see, during your life on earth, you had certain tasks to accomplish and we need to examine these life lessons to see if you did indeed learn them. If there is evidence you didn't, then we examine your life in more detail, and see how and why you missed out on the opportunities. When all this is done you're allowed to move onwards, and then the next part of your work will be to decide the lessons you are to learn in your next life."

"You are talking the same nonsense I had to hear from Jacqueline and her friends. You cannot *possibly* mean that my beliefs are wrong after all these years. You're turning the Day of Judgement into something resembling a therapy, and I *won't* have it!"

The little man's face fell. As Sonia turned her back, another prayer silently formed itself on his lips.

> *Dear God,*
> *please give me the wisdom to choose the right words - and the*
> *strength to continue.*
> *Amen.*

Aloud, he said,

"What you can't remember is that this is a process that you've done before - when you've left one Earthly life you've returned here, then moved on to a new one in order to improve your soul's understanding. As you probably know, the word for this is Reincarnation.

"I know in your last earthly life you enjoyed keeping a journal, so I've provided you with one here. As well as that, I'd like you to make a start on the lessons. Usually people are asked to list the Ten Commandments and explain how they have observed them. But with you we will try something more refined and intellectually befitting."

Sonia was about to try another bout of huffiness, but somewhat mollified by the implied compliment of recognising that her knowledge was above the ordinary, decided to keep quiet.

"There's no hurry" he continued "just let your thoughts flow into your journal, and in the meantime you'll have the best of everything brought to you – ask and it will be provided, as we always say. For now, I suggest you take another walk in the garden and enjoy the chance to rest while you can."

It was some time before Sonia came back to her room, and looking around saw no sign of the little man. Breathing a sigh of relief, she crossed to her desk. A journal lay in front of her – the new one, bought for her 76th year, and surely there could never be a better time to start it. She sat down reached for her pen and started to write, hoping to feel the peace and pleasure she had always felt as she consigned her thoughts, hopes and wishes to paper, as if to her dearest friend.

The journal of Sonia, Lady Woolston, of Woolston Hall, near Guildford, Surrey.

Apparently I have died. This seems an utterly ridiculous statement to make, but I have now been shown incontrovertible proof that it is indeed so, and I must accept it.

I will admit I was a little taken aback when I learned I had to have a companion with whom to share my thoughts, but he has provided this, my journal, and I will insist that my privacy be respected. If this ever gets discovered it should make fascinating reading ….

I am in a large house of some sort, which has been made to feel like my drawing room as far as possible, although the architecture here is very strange. There are no ceilings, so when I refer to a doorway I mean an opening between two pillars whose tops are shrouded in far distant gossamer cloud. Quite beautiful. There is no need for practicality here, of course, as there is apparently an even climate.

The garden is a delight, although I have only explored a small part of it so far. The little stream is perfect. It emerges from under the steps that lead down from the doorway, sparkling and glinting in this special light that is so bright, yet does not make one's eyes ache. It tumbles down among grassy banks and over pebbles that look as polished as any semi-precious stone.

If Jacqueline were here with me, no doubt she could identify each and every one, and bore me to tears with the so-called healing properties they are supposed to have. Such nonsense, I once told her – the only properties they have are to provide comfort to those who believe the mumbo jumbo. Only precious stones are worth polishing and should be set in precious metals, to be admired, and worn with discretion.

But I digress ...

Looking around me I can see many flowers that I do not recognise. How interesting, and how my friends in the Ladies Gardening Club would beg me for cuttings if only I could take some back. The gardens seem to be haphazard in their design, which surprises me – I would have thought that things would be more ordered, somehow. There are some areas which are most definitely overgrown, too, but perhaps they give scope for those who wish to perpetuate their earthly pursuits.

Apparently this place is called the Review Centre. They have recreated my drawing room so that I feel completely at ease. I have been told by the little man (who, incidentally, suggested I call him "Master" – such nonsense – I informed him I would name him Mister Fu, as he looks vaguely Oriental) that when I feel ready, we can start on a task of great significance.

From what I can gather at this stage, we are all born into a life where we have the opportunity to improve ourselves. The task is to look at one's achievements and discuss them. When this Mister Fu is satisfied (which I cannot imagine will be too difficult, as my achievements speak for themselves), I will pass to another stage for what I can only regard as some sort of recycling process of my soul. Another life ahead? Will I remember all this? I will keep this journal to record whatever happens and try to take it with me, if indeed I do return to another life on earth.

All this nonsense about how I lived my life and how I affected others will quickly be sorted out when he learns how I fought for my position in society and retained it, in spite of many handicaps. I was always engaged in good works of one sort or another, and the donations I made, or ordered Geoffrey to make on my behalf, will keep any recording angel very happy for a very long time, if one is judged by the gratitude one receives in life.

As for personal achievements, I hardly know where to begin, there are so many throughout my life. In fact it seems to have been one long spell of success after another – overcoming my childhood illnesses, marrying the man who gave me the potential to enter the lifestyle I could foresee as my destiny – and yes, I know I made the most of that potential – socially and financially.

56

Geoffrey had his share of the bargain too, of course, and I was wholeheartedly devoted to him for all those years, even when I discovered what he was pleased to call his "little indiscretion". (Hopefully we will not need to discuss that).

But I run ahead of myself and there is no place for that in my new journal, so it is certainly time to change the current of my thoughts, and after another rest I will begin to write what the wretched man wants. Then perhaps I can move on before I get too bored with the whole thing.

Mr Fu was also writing. He sent a memo to God:

Dear God –
To be quite honest, when I received the summons I thought 'You've managed to do it again!' -
I know I did a good job with all those other formidable ladies, but I really don't wish to make a career of it!

When it was nearly time for Lady Sonia to enter the Afterlife, I thought I'd prepared myself thoroughly, but I will admit to some qualms as she came over. As part of fitting in with whatever my recently-passed-over human related to in their Earthly life, I've chosen to get her started on a journal. The first exercise will be a good way to find out the scope of her self-delusions.
I've already realised there will be no point in being too gentle with Lady Sonia or she would treat me as arrogantly as she has treated most living people. No doubt there will be tantrums, and she may try to bother You with small matters. I can only apologise in advance.
All will be well eventually – as You know.

Your most devoted Worshipper -
Angel Prince of the East, Master of the Higher Realms.

(Now also known as 'Mr Fu'!)

⇥9⇤

NOT SURPRISINGLY, THE ATMOSPHERE AT Woolston Hall was tense in every respect, whichever permutation of family or staff encountered each other.

"Thank goodness we have our work to get on with" Doris said to Annie several times in the next day or two "even though I seem to be catering for people with no appetite, or who are liable to leave the table at a moment's notice."

"They're having to handle all sorts" Annie agreed. "Routine's impossible."

It would be even more unlikely when Victoria and the baby returned from the hospital. The Nanny would be arriving soon and would need to be settled in and catered for. Doris's work was now punctured by many sighs. The hours seemed endless and the funeral date had yet to be set, although it seemed that it was unlikely to be this side of the New Year.

Annie busied herself keeping out of Benjamin's way as much as possible, except at mealtimes – she did not want to be at his beck and call. The task of sorting Sonia's clothes and carefully packing them away between layers of tissue paper, in boxes that George then took up to one of the attic rooms, could take some time to complete. The jewellery had gone straight into the safe, of course, a few pieces awaiting dispersal to various homes as part of the distribution that would take place when Sonia's Last Will and Testament was made public knowledge.

Ben realised that he would have to spend many days, if not weeks, getting back into Vicky's good books. Although there had been his apology, and her apparent acceptance, in the hospital, he knew he would have to tread warily for a time. What a fool he had been - but totally justified at the time, he thought, on his second night in the Library in front of the fire with the

59

brandy at his elbow. He slumped morosely into the leather chair unable to do anything other than focus on his loss, unable to summon the mental resources to shoulder any more responsibilities for that day.

The door opening made him start, but when he saw it was Barbara he relaxed and vaguely waved a hand towards the drinks cabinet in the corner of the room.

"Help yourself, Auntie Babs" he slurred "it's all yours at the moment. Things will change, of course, when my wonderful doting wife returns complete with nappies, bottles, potties, prams, buggies and sacks full of clothes. No more drinkies then for the Daddy, so make the most of it." He slumped further into his chair, and Barbara wondered how many drinks he had consumed since dinner.

"How is the baby?" she enquired. "Are you and Victoria any nearer choosing a name yet? Or several?"

"D'you know, Babs, it never occurred to me to think of girls' names. All I could think of was that it would be a boy. Vicky didn't want to know beforehand, said it was unlucky, so we didn't take up the offer when they did the umpteenth scan. Wish I'd known so I could have got used to the idea – keep wanting to call it Charlie!"

"Don't do anything so foolish, for heaven's sake. You're in your wife's bad books as it is. These days, not being there for the birth is a black mark against *any* father, let alone not turning up until the following morning, *and* with a monumental hangover. You're going to have to buy something very special for your wife to get rid of those memories."

She poured herself a drink, waved the heavy decanter enquiringly in Ben's direction, and receiving a response, walked across to top up his glass. She was now wondering if it had really been a good idea to volunteer to stay through the intervening days between now and the funeral, but felt that she might somehow be a stabilising influence. It could be a last tribute to her lifelong friend. But for all her composure, Barbara too was in shock. Fifty years of friendship was not to be dismissed lightly.

"You know" she mused to a half-aware Benjamin, attempting to change to a different subject, but one that might arouse his interest. "I never thought when your mother invited me for the first business weekend all those years ago that it would lead to such success. Sonia certainly had a flair for entertaining and making sure that everything went smoothly. She'd done smaller things before they moved here, of course, but this house was the perfect setting for exclusive negotiations. Even when you children had arrived, it all carried on like clockwork. Victoria will be doing the same, no doubt, with the conferences you're planning?"

Ben grunted.

"She'd better not try to wriggle out of it. Mother groomed her and spent hours going over every little detail of every event – she kept detailed diaries, you know. Pretty remarkable woman, my mother … oh God, I *miss* her … I don't know how we … "

Barbara knew that Ben was close to his mother, but the anguish and panic in his voice alarmed her with its intensity.

"*You* have to be the head of the household, so you must *not* go to pieces. Drinking won't help, either, you know, although you'll be excused for a day or two longer before people begin to fear the worst. Now tell me what you propose doing about the Nanny."

Ben twisted in his chair, but Barbara's brisk tone made him drag his scattered thoughts together. No use antagonising her as well, he realised, so he resentfully outlined the plan.

"She's been contacted and can come earlier than planned, after all. When she arrives the day after tomorrow, I take her to the hospital to meet Vic, then everything will be set up here for them both to return when the brat's got the all clear from the medics – turns out she wasn't as premature as we'd all thought, but not enough to start tongues wagging in the village."

So that was it, Barbara thought, remembering the haste with which the wedding plans had been put into action. Those months of Sonia intensively coaching Victoria in how to run the Hall made sense now - done in case she might not be interested, or even have time to learn, after the birth. No wonder poor Sonia had looked pale by the time it was her birthday.

Barbara lit another cigarette and let her thoughts silently wander, making no pretence of prolonging conversation with Ben. So that was the way the wind blew – he had no confidence in Victoria's commitment to the business plans, and no wonder. Certainly she was a girl Barbara found it difficult to warm to – no generosity in her manner, and a sulky sullenness when she was thwarted that did her no favours at all. Maybe she would rally round when it eventually dawned on her that she was mistress of the Hall, and it was her responsibility to ensure that things carried on.

Barbara felt a foreboding about the future that she could not shake off – of family harmony, and of the Hall and all it stood for. Would she herself continue to be seen as helpful or would Ben's wife see her as interfering? What a sad end to a family of whom she had grown so fond … but then she mentally shook herself – what nonsense to look on the negative side when there was also so much potential. Of course things would not be the same – but it did not have to be the worst scenario: it had the potential to change for the better, particularly if she could make herself indispensable. She too could adapt to whatever lay ahead if she just took her own advice and tackled one day at a time, concentrating on whatever task she undertook.

><

Jacqueline's kitchen was warm and bright. Outside, Boxing Day's hard frost had covered everywhere in a sparkle of candy coating, the winter sun was casting its light across the lawn and the birds were already busy at the bird table. It lifted her spirits immeasurably. Richard was eating his usual toast and honey, while the children still slept on. They had hardly stirred when they were eventually carried up to bed, and although Jacqui had spent the night sleeping fitfully in order to hear the slightest murmur, it was not Tim or Ella who caused her restlessness. She worried about her brother and how he would be able to adjust – not only to the massive changes that fatherhood would bring, but also to the fact that Sonia would no longer be there to maintain a steering role at the Hall.

Richard needed to go to the Practice for a short time, on duty to see any emergency patients, although there were rarely too many of those just after Christmas, and as there were no house calls booked it meant that he would be back by lunchtime. They could all go for a walk after lunch, she thought, smiling across at him over the rim of her cup. In response to his enquiring look she responded.

"I continue to think that I must be the luckiest woman in the country to have met you."

"What's wrong with the whole world?" he teased. "You've demoted me in a sentence!"

"You understand so much, yet you hardly had a chance to get to know my mother properly."

"Put it down to my renowned bedside manner, darling, and please can we have some of your famous soup when I return – all that heavy Christmas food is lying like a lead weight!"

He blew her a kiss as he swung cheerily out of the door, then returned to tilt her head towards him.

"And don't take any nonsense from that brother of yours - refer him to me if he wants you to do too much. By all means go there for a day or two before the funeral if it would help, providing I'm there with you – I'll phone my parents straight away to see if they can look after the children here. No more than that, though" he added firmly " *you* have to have time to adjust, too."

Jacqui smiled up at him appreciatively and started the chores, thinking about what was to come. They knew about the technicalities that might mean the funeral could not be sanctioned until the authorities were satisfied that nothing improper had taken place. Fortunately her mother had seen Dr

Hartley not too long ago, over a minor matter, so once offices were open after the holiday arrangements could be made and people notified.

She wondered how things were at the Hall. Ben was not the best person to rise to a crisis – his mother was the one who had always steered him through anything unpleasant, but at least Barbara was there to help. Jacqui loved her brother in spite of the way his attitudes sometimes betrayed the effects of Sonia's unfair bias and favouritism. Underneath his 'must be top dog and centre of attention at all times' attitude she knew he was and always had been very fond of her. Once, when even his beloved mother had overstepped the boundaries and yet again punished Jacqueline unfairly, he had interceded on his sister's behalf.

"*Don't* interfere with what you don't understand" Sonia had snapped - with such fury that he had hidden in the attic for the rest of the day. When Jacqui found him she made him promise not to do it again – she was used to the regime and felt she was tougher than Ben. It still mystified her. There was not, and never had been, any obvious explanation for Sonia's attitude. Fortunately, Jacqui had been protected by her father's love, and remembered him with the huge sense of loss that six years had done nothing to lessen.

She felt deeply saddened that her relationship with her mother had never been better than a thinly disguised veil of tolerance on Sonia's part. When Jacqui had been betrayed yet again by her first husband Zak and decided to divorce him, it was to friends she was forced to turn for help and support as a single mother. Sonia ignored her for many months. Having disapproved of the marriage in the first place, she was not going to play any supportive role in its painful end, and certainly had no wish to provide accommodation at the Hall for either her daughter or her infant grandson. When the publicity died down and the public's interest in picking over the excesses of yet another pop musician, Jacqueline was eventually allowed to resume contact and Sonia never again mentioned the marriage.

When Jacqui remarried, Sonia tolerated Anthony because any branch of medicine was a respectable profession, even though she herself was wary of psychologists. The thought of his additional skills in hypnotherapy made her wince – not for *her* this dabbling about in people's minds; but it paid well enough and Anthony himself was charming. His death had been so totally unexpected, yet the news that Jacqueline was expecting his child helped them as they grieved.

Those had been very dark days, when she had more than once wondered how anything could ever be worthwhile again. But incredibly it proved to be the start of a sequence of events that had led to the eventual meeting with Richard, briefly standing in as practice locum doctor. The healing began and they both carefully built a relationship that they knew would stand the test of time. Sonia's death was the first major crisis life had given them since their marriage, although already Jacqui knew her confidence in Richard was well founded. She poured another cup of coffee and waited for sounds that the children were waking, wanting a diversion from her thoughts.

Sure enough, before long the children crept downstairs, rubbing their eyes and yawning. With the resilience of the very young, they were soon engrossed in their presents, then Ella organised Tim into a game of Nonny playing with the angels which meant a lot of racing around up and down stairs with arms outstretched.

When Jacqueline phoned to speak to her brother, Barbara took the call and became quite emotional. Jacqui had been the first to ask how *she* was feeling, and show genuine concern.

"I shall feel much better when all this is over" admitted Barbara when her voice became steady once again "but at least there's plenty of practical work to do. Are you able to come here before the day of the funeral? I know it's a cheek to even ask, but I also know it will help so much, as Victoria will be busy with the baby."

"Richard's parents will be having the children for as long as necessary, bless them, so we can both be at the Hall for a couple of days to do anything that's needed. Poor Ben, he's got so much on his plate."

"Poor Ben needs steering away from the brandy decanter at the moment" Barbara replied tartly "and to be perfectly frank, I'm not the one to help him with that – I've had more years of practice than he has!"

"I'm sure it will all settle down. Don't be too hard on him – or *you*, for that matter. It's time for lunch, so I'll have to leave you for now. I'll be in touch every evening if you need some moral support or anything else, but do feel you can phone at *any* other time – whether you want help, or just a chat."

The family afternoon passed with much healthy exercise and laughter. The children adored Richard, and he them, and their time together was always full of fun. It just proved how life can and must go on, Jacqui thought, no matter how devastating the circumstances; and in the scale of things, she felt so much more able to cope with her mother's death. Sonia had at least reached her biblical 'three score years and ten', whereas Anthony had been cheated of that fullness of time.

Some semblance of routine resumed at the Hall. Ben visited Victoria in the late afternoons, having spent office hours dealing with the myriad aspects of officialdom and paperwork necessary to steer events to their conclusion. Weekends and official holidays made this the worst time of year for a death in one way, but it gave the family some much needed breathing space. The date for the funeral was set for the fourth day of January, announcements were made in the newspapers, letters were written to all Sonia's contacts who would need to know. There was the dreadful poignancy that the contact list was the one Sonia herself had so recently used for the scores of Christmas cards.

Ben had decided to make amends to his wife, at Barbara's prompting, and had rushed to a jeweller's in Guildford as soon as it reopened. An exquisite gold necklace set with pearls and small amethysts seemed to be the ideal gift for Victoria – both to mark their daughter's birth, and also to get back in her good books.

Victoria had confided in a senior member of the nursing staff at the hospital, explaining her misery at Ben's immediate reaction to the arrival of a daughter instead of the planned-for son. Ben had been called into a private meeting to be firmly made aware that he had to be careful to guard his comments, and he genuinely determined to turn over a new leaf and become the exemplary new father. Nanny had been contacted and was due to arrive almost immediately. It was as well that arrangements for the nursery suite at the Hall had been completed well before the end of October - so that it would not interfere with the birthday preparations, of course, and as another example of the planning and organisation in which Sonia had revelled. She had also interviewed the Nanny, and Clair Frost had come with the highest recommendations. She was a mature and experienced Nanny who would be able to handle the most delicate situations, and although secretly a little frightened of her, Vicky knew she and the baby would be in safe hands.

Working together in the kitchen gave Annie and Doris plenty of time to speculate on how Victoria would fare in her late mother-in-law's shoes. Doris had found her willing enough to learn the routines, but out of her depth when it came to understanding the finer nuances of household management. On the occasions when Sonia had left her to take responsibility, Victoria tried to cover her own inadequacies with an autocratic manner that was often infuriating and always unnecessary. Doris was the one mostly on the receiving end, which she correctly attributed to nervousness on Victoria's part, but nonetheless it caused many silent smarts. The worst occasion had been when she attempted to cover an oversight on her own part by blaming Doris for lack of co-operation, but fortunately Sonia had, at least publicly, ignored that. Whether or not she had privately taken Victoria to task over the issue had of course never been revealed, but Doris had been very indignant.

Annie and Doris took to spending time in the evenings at the gatehouse, after dinner. Their friendship developed a new closeness that had not been possible before, when their duties tended to give them time off separately. In any case, Sonia would have firmly taken steps to discourage too much familiarity between the housekeeper and her personal companion.

"When the funeral's over I'm going to insist on being called by my full name at long last" Annie said during a conversation on the first evening they were on their own. "I've always hated Annie more than I can say!"

Doris was startled.

"D'you know, I'd forgotten about that. When you were in the village I always thought Annabel was the prettiest name, but why did you change it if you didn't like it?

"Sonia did that. Told me it was too pretentious for someone who had no cause to have airs and graces, and that Annie was a traditional servant's name."

"I know it was many years ago and attitudes have changed, but how could you agree?"

"I suppose I was having some sort of breakdown - the Vicar's wife and Lady Sonia got me sorted out between them. Looking back, I must have been too weak to argue, but anyway, nobody argues with her Ladyship, do they? Sorry - argued – so I agreed to anything. It was a better post than I had at the school, after all, and it eventually led to more than I could have ever dreamed would be possible."

She lapsed into silence, and Doris assumed she was referring to the benefits of being a Lady's companion, compared with the mundane routine of supervising the infants' class. Annabelle, however, was silently, wistfully, remembering passion and excitement, secrecy and intrigue.

"One day I'll tell you the whole story, Doris, but not now – not yet."

And with that her friend had to be content.

✥10✥

"MISTER FU! – I CANNOT get accustomed to your gliding up behind me, nor do I intend to. Please do not make a habit of it in future!"

Lady Sonia had decided that if there was no way of avoiding the obnoxious little man, as she thought of him, and that she did indeed have to do the work he had set, the best way of handling him was to keep him in his place – which of course would be as she had always treated the least significant people in her life.

"Dear Lady Sonia - I just wanted to say that I'm so pleased you've started recording things in your little journal, but we'll soon need to begin the serious work – the first Task. It's only when these Tasks have been done, that we can look at your life and see if we can uncover the details of how you have learned your lessons."

Sonia bridled. He sounded positively patronising about her journal – and no-one, but *no-one*, had ever dared to patronise her and lived to tell the tale. He really was quite awful, yet he was apparently her only contact in this place, so rather than be left in solitude she decided to try to be reasonably pleasant.

"Lessons? You sound like my wretched daughter and the sort of thinking she dabbled with. The church taught me that I was put on earth to achieve, and to make use of my talents, and surely I have done that over and over again, benefiting countless other people. I have always believed in leading from the front and setting an example to which others may aspire. I also learned that when I died, providing I had led a virtuous life, I could expect a long blissful rest waiting for the Resurrection Day, when all the great and the good will find themselves together for evermore. Naturally, I expect to be one of that assembly. It will take me a long time, if ever, to get used to this situation, and I still cannot understand why everything is so different."

Oh dear Lord, he thought, that self-righteousness will have to go before anything else, and it's going to be so painful for her. But she will have to do it, or she will never believe what she sees and the result will be that the next stage will have less effect. There was no use trying to hurry the process. He'd had many stubborn people through his hands since time began, and although he pretended to grumble when another came his way, he really found a great deal of satisfaction in accompanying them through a difficult time, then seizing the moment when arrogance turned to humility and rewarding it with kindness and peace. In the meantime he would have to be firm – even stern, or she would inevitably try to overrule him.

"Dear lady, you'll find there have been many simplistic notions over the centuries, fed by leaders to the masses, in order to keep them happy and in their place. Heads of organisations always do this, and heads of various religions no less so. Now – I'd like you to do the first written exercise for me. It will have to be done before you can move on."

"Oh no, I have met you so-called Socialist thinkers before - all you can think about are the downtrodden masses and it is utter nonsense! The masses have to have leaders; people of my status are natural leaders; it is the natural order of civilisation. Now, if there truly *is* no alternative, I am prepared to do something that helps to make sense of why I am here, which will allow me to move on to where I *should* be, but before we start I must point out that I will retain my faith and trust in the teachings of the Church I know, come what may."

He ignored her protestations and folded his hands under his robe.

"I'm here to help you understand how it all fits in with the greater scheme of things and it will become clearer as we do the work. The first task will simple – I'll give you one of the Great Laws which tell how people are expected to interact with one another in their Earthly life; then I'd like you to pen your thoughts on how it has been part of your own life, and how it has affected those around you."

"I have no fears about any of your laws" retorted Sonia "I am sure I will have heard of them, and if, as you say, they are foundations of life, then I can expect them to fit in with any teachings of the Church to which I have adhered."

Mr Fu produced a small scroll from the sleeve of his robe and unfurling it, read aloud a short statement.

"Do as you would have others do unto you."

"Well?" Sonia asked, expecting more.

"That is the first one - nothing more, nothing less."

"But this is infantile!"

"Well, yes – you see we need to go back to the beginning. All the examples you can think of, and also how they affected those involved. Please do as I ask, dear lady. Contemplate the statement deeply and you will find the true implications. Don't be taken in by the simplicity, because in this, and the other tasks that I shall give you later, lies the whole purpose of life."

Sonia sat at her desk with the scroll in her hands long after Mr Fu had departed. It was typical! She was willing to expound her theories and argue her points, exercising her intellect as indeed she had done on many committees and in many meetings throughout her life. Now here was this dreadful little man taking away all that fun, bringing her to the very basics and depriving her of the opportunity to impress him with her erudition.

Well, as a first exercise it was going to be easy enough, thought Sonia, and there was nothing else to do with her time. She copied the sentence into her journal.

"Do as you would have others do unto you."

She wrote pages. She wrote of hospitality, of generous gifts. She described acts of unparalleled magnanimity until Mr Fu returned, just in time to witness the last graceful flourish of her pen, then laying it down, she turned to him triumphantly.

"There you are – now may we please move on?"

He read her work thoughtfully, pacing the room as he read, sometimes shaking his head with a rueful expression, sometimes frowning, then sent up a silent prayer that he might be guided to choose the most tactful words for what he had to say next.

"I do appreciate the insights you've given me, dear Lady Sonia, but I'm afraid it's unfinished. These are just examples of things you were able to do because of your wealth. Were people's lives made better by exchanging expensive gifts on an escalating scale? Also, I did ask you to describe what the consequences of these acts were - in the lives of all those they affected."

"I should have thought it was obvious!" she retorted. "They were all without fail exceedingly grateful, and yes, they did find ways of repaying me, for which I also expressed gratitude in due course. It is the current commerce of friends and acquaintances at any level."

"I don't doubt that, but please remember we're looking at what ties in with a true principle of life, not these current so-called civilised ideas.

"Perhaps we should make it even simpler - tell me about something you once did for no other purpose than that of being kind; then maybe we can discuss the results together."

Sonia wondered whether to argue the point, but reluctantly picked up her pen again. After a great deal of cudgelling, her brain eventually remembered a very minor event from the past that she had forgotten years ago and would nowadays dismiss as nonsense – a moment of what she shamefacedly thought of as weakness, and had forever kept secret, when she impulsively thrust a ten pound note into a street musician's box, just because a tune reminded her of a happy moment in childhood.

Mr Fu was much more delighted with this than with the pages of notes she had written out before.

"But I cannot say *how* it affected that man's life, because I never saw him again!" she said, puzzled.

"That's just the point, you *don't* know for certain, so it was an act of true generosity. Whenever we work in that way it becomes a demonstration of faith in the Higher Powers. Would you like to know what happened?"

Curiosity aroused, she nodded before she could stop herself.

"The musician treated his friends to a drink ..."

Sonia snorted contemptuously.

"No, no – let me finish: he had reached a really low point that day when you walked past, and his self-esteem was practically non-existent. What you did gave him renewed faith in himself and he was able to hold his head up high and treat his friends, rather than being dependent on handouts. That proved to be a turning point in his life – he saw that he wanted to be able to do that every day. He realised that if he could play that well when he was at his lowest point, he might be even better if he worked hard at his music. He made up his mind not to waste his life, went on to join a group and eventually began to earn a real living wage. Nowadays he's training other drop-outs to use their musical skills."

"Is this really true?"

Mr Fu nodded vigorously.

"This is why it's such an important idea – it's never simply the deed itself, but its repercussions that spread like ripples in a pond, after a pebble has been dropped in. Now please record that in your book so that they may be referred to again."

Sonia, surprising herself, did as she was told. However, the success of approval prompted her to ask about the next Law. Knowing this would be much more difficult, and too much haste would lead to a need for painful proof, Mr Fu attempted to abide by his decision that it was not quite time for the project. Of course, this led to trouble - she tried to insist, he resisted, she fumed and would not be swayed.

Eventually, after getting close to offering up a heartfelt prayer to be delivered from the task, he decided it might be used to prove a point, and somewhat reluctantly produced the next scroll from his sleeve.

"I warn you, dear lady, that unless you approach this task with the greatest humility, you could be very disturbed by the consequences."

"Why - is there trickery in this one?" Sonia asked suspiciously.

"No trickery at all - this is just the other side of the coin, so to speak."

He handed her the small scroll, with the words

'As you sow, so shall you reap.'

"This time I want you to apply the subject to attitudes – both your own and other people's. Think hard about other people you have known and worked with, and be honest – have you *really* been aware of their true attitudes towards you, or have you made assumptions?

"It's an idea that should start you thinking of *how* people treated you in your Earthly life in the way that they did, and more importantly, *why.*

"Your last visit produced some surprises and has maybe started you wondering if you know everyone as well as you think you do? Have you always listened to what people want, or have you imposed your own will? Have you encouraged people to use their initiative, or have you kept them in their place?"

Sonia frowned. This was taking her into deeper waters than she cared to admit. But then she straightened herself in the chair, remembering how she had, in the past, made even bishops and cabinet ministers quail with her sharp thinking (and even sharper tongue when necessary) – so she, of all people, would not be intimidated by a shabby little man, whatever fancy titles he gave himself.

He left her to mull over her thoughts while he wrote out his next report, prefaced by a memo:

Dear God –
Sonia has a phenomenal tendency to argue things out to suit

herself! Hearing people's <u>true</u> opinions may be the only way to prove that she is mistaken, however upset she becomes. As ever, I shall continue to seek signs of humility, before moving to the next stage.
Thank you for answering my prayers –
as always, your Angel, Fu

Time was non-existent of course, so it could have been hours, or even days later, measured by Earth time - Sonia was still sitting there, deep in thought - when Mr Fu returned. Nothing had been added to the second statement she had copied from the scroll.

"As you sow, so shall you reap!" she quoted, sneeringly. "You wretched man! This means nothing to me! I have spent a lifetime of giving and yes, I have received service in return – that is what wages are for, although it would appear that some have forgotten that simple fact, judging by the behaviour of Annie and Doris."

"Are you really having such great difficulty seeing yourself as others saw you? Have you received willing service? If not – why? Could it be that you have taken advantage of your position as employer and exploited those who have no choice?"

Sonia started to look mutinous, so he changed tack.

"Let us think of something else – forgiveness. Has there been a time when you felt you'd been let down or something really bad happened, and you wanted revenge in some way."

Sonia immediately shuddered.

"My father - he betrayed my mother and abandoned me."

"Ah, precisely so - and did you ever forgive him?"

"Forgiveness? My mother never let me speak his name again. She was bitter and hated him, so I naturally followed suit."

"But did you actually *want* to do that? Forget what your mother wanted you to do - did *you* ever try to get in touch with him later on, to hear his side of things?"

"Well, I did wonder once or twice, I suppose, then I was too busy getting my own life sorted out. I eventually heard he had died years ago, so of course it was too late by then. I think he used to send me birthday cards, but my mother hid them and I only found one by accident when I was clearing out some old papers."

She looked almost wistful for a moment, then became her normal brisk self again.

"What good would forgiveness have done? We wanted him to suffer as we had done, reaping what *he* had sowed" she added triumphantly, expecting to have scored a point and prepared to encounter an argument she felt she would eventually win. But her strategy was transparent.

"Exactly – that's just what can happen! But I want you to think about the possible positive aspects if you had met? You *could* have attempted to understand, and in doing that, everyone concerned would have had the chance to forgive and heal old wounds. Life is all about opportunities to perpetuate good, and undo bad. Your suffering was just as prolonged as your father's, just as wasteful, and achieved nothing but bitterness that damaged all concerned."

Sonia flung down her pen in a fit of bad temper and stalked out into the garden. Some of this was going to get very uncomfortable, she realised. If only there was a way out of this wretched 'work' as he called it. If only she could see her own darling Benjamin again and remind herself of how a parent and child relationship could and should be.

The more she thought, the more she longed to do that. Could she, dare she, ask for another trip to the Hall? The last visit had been awful, seeing and hearing Annie and Doris betraying her and plotting now she was gone, after she had shown them nothing but kindness over the years. How did Mr Fu's theory fit in with their behaviour? But seeing Benjamin would provide her with the reassurance she needed. He would be grieving, but would also be strong and dependable – a son to be proud of, demonstrating what her training could achieve.

Mr Fu appeared, as if he read her very thoughts. Although he knew what she was about to ask, he also knew what would be the consequence. So be it – he would be there, as he always was and had been.

"We will put aside the work until later, dear lady – I think you've done enough for now, and I didn't intend to upset you. Are you certain it's to be Benjamin this time?"

Sonia nodded. The thought of seeing her beloved son, yet not being able to speak any words of comfort to him was almost too much to bear, but she steeled herself to be content with whatever peace of mind it brought to her, and prepared herself for what was now becoming a familiar transition from the Afterlife to an Earthly location – the speed and the soft wings.

This time it proved to be her son's bedroom and Victoria was sitting on the bed, sobbing.

"I do hope that girl is not going to be a dreadful disappointment" thought Sonia from her vantage point at the far side of the room. She had hoped that Victoria would by now be showing signs of her mother-in-law's own dignity and ability to hide undue signs of emotional upset. "After all those talks I gave her on how to put on a brave face and disguise her feelings, now here she is, snivelling at some imaginary little problem. Ah, that's better," she thought, seeing Victoria start at hearing Ben come into the bedroom, and moving swiftly to the stool at the dressing table, pretend to be engrossed in brushing her hair.

Ben sat down on the bed and asked how the baby had been. How thoughtful, Sonia thought – her son was such a tender loving husband.

"I'm not seeing very much of her. Clair keeps telling me I need to rest, so I only see her at feeding times."

"Nanny knows best, they always say, so for heaven's sake stop moaning."

"It's all very well for you – you were brought up by one, so it's normal, I suppose. We didn't have that, and I can't get used to the idea. It feels as if she's not my baby at all."

"Look, we're paying a great deal of money for her. Clair came highly recommended and we agreed that we would do it this way. Anyway, you're obviously getting back to normal, so the sooner you help with all the work, the better. Now, we must choose the names, because I may as well register her birth when I collect Mummy's certificate."

Victoria shuddered.

"I know she was born the same day as your mother died, but do you *really* have to be so tactless?" Her voice rose, hysterical tears not far away. "Is that old witch's death going to haunt her for the rest of her life, so that she can never have a birthday without us all being reminded of it?"

Ben strode across the room and taking her by the shoulders, turned her round on the stool to face him. Bending low and menacingly, he looked fiercely into her eyes.

"Don't ever – *ever* – speak like that of the woman who gave me everything. You are fortunate that you received her approval and that somehow she saw in you an eventual worthy successor. Because you are my wife, you will act like the wife I need and be a testimony to my mother's judgement and training. If you feel you can't live up to those standards you may as well pack your bags and leave at once - and don't imagine I'd lose much sleep over that! I'm rapidly getting tired of your miserable whining about how difficult everything is – get up and actually do something useful, for once in your life!"

Victoria cringed under his grip and looked aside, but he roughly cupped her chin, forcing her to look directly at him as he spoke.

"Now – we will have Sonia as one name, of course, Margaret for my father's mother's memory, and that leaves you with the main choice. See how generous I am when you start to behave?"

Victoria managed to draw breath and tremulously said "Lucinda."

Ben squeezed her jaw viciously, then contemptuously withdrew his hand, strode out of the room and returned to the Library, his inevitable refuge away from baby noises and his wife's tantrums.

Sonia was appalled, yet there must be something that justified it – undoubtedly something his wife had done that had driven him beyond human endurance. She looked down at the dejected new mother and muttered darkly to herself.

"You cannot even begin to know unhappiness, compared with mine. Pull yourself together and make an effort – if I could climb my mountain, then you can surely cope with this molehill! Mr Fu – we shall return, I have seen enough!"

But Mr Fu had other ideas and, determined to let the point be made in as explicit a way as possible, he took the unwilling Lady Sonia downstairs to the Library.

✦11✦

BARBARA HAD FOUND PLENTY TO do, supervising the arrangements for the funeral gathering in just over a week's time. Replies and condolences had been pouring in since the public announcements, and she fielded the media questions with skill – not in order to protect Ben, but simply to do the job effectively. She could not trust him to handle the press in the right way, even though all they wanted was a summary of Sonia's local achievements. The danger of an over-zealous reporter just happening to ask one too many questions might prove to be too much, particularly if he had been hiding in the Library, where she knew he kept the reserve supplies of brandy, and it was preferable to be cautious.

Her own needs continued to be propped up by regular but discreet consumption of alcohol, and supplies of her favourite slender cigarillos – although as a concession to the presence of the baby in the house, her smoking was confined to the Library, where often her need for escape coincided with Ben's.

"Have you noticed anything wrong with the heating?" Victoria asked that evening, joining them after dinner. She had eventually overcome her weeping sufficiently to feel she needed company – any company, even in that atmosphere. "It doesn't always work effectively. Sometimes I feel really cold in some rooms, but it appears to be fine in the nursery."

"Oh, as long as *that's* all right" Ben looked viciously at his wife, still in the aftermath of his earlier bad mood. "We could have howling gales blowing through every nook and cranny and no-one would turn a hair, just as long as the *nursery's* not affected. Of course, it could just be my mother coming back to haunt you – has *that* occurred to you?"

79

Sonia wondered fleetingly whether she could indeed be seen in the corner behind the desk, but a small chuckle from Mr Fu made her realise it was impossible.

Barbara decided to ignore Ben's sarcasm and eventually his moody silence started to ease as the brandy took effect. With the decanter passing between Barbara and Ben – Victoria forced to abstain because of feeding the baby – they became reflective, and talk turned to speculating about Sonia and her childhood. Victoria asked Barbara how she and Sonia had become friends, although she had heard Sonia's version; but it was a safe topic of conversation, and she was beginning to realise how friendless she was in this household – better to get into Barbara's good books rather than antagonise her. Ben slumped lower in his chair and soon the drone of voices lulled him into sleep.

"It spans several decades, but it's not a long story. You probably know that we both came from the same town – and in fact had attended the same school, although four years difference in our ages meant that we did not meet there. No, that was not to happen until my first secretarial post at Woolston Manufacturing - Geoffrey's father's firm. Although Sonia was by then already rather grand, we got on well and she enjoyed training me as much as I enjoyed learning. Well, when she and Geoffrey got married it broke many hearts, but it was a wise choice for him. Her father knew her capabilities so the marriage received his blessing, and he hoped it would settle his son down. Too many sailors found life very tame after the War ended, you see, but with a wife and a good business, Geoffrey could turn his energies to helping his father."

"Did it work out like that?"

"Oh yes. Well, at least on the surface. The truth was, Sonia was very, *very* ambitious. Now that's a great asset when your husband is due to inherit the fruits of his father's labours. Geoffrey was used to travel, so it was natural that he should take over the sales side and Sonia decided she could develop the contacts he made, so that their business clients became social and loyal friends. She did it very cleverly, of course, so that their large family home retained an air of a privileged club, and when they moved down here to the Hall, the most favoured were invited to the weekends."

These occasional weekend gatherings – no more than six each year, Sonia had informed Victoria as part of her grooming to become the hostess of similar events - had been extremely successful, as much because of their exclusivity as the actual events themselves. It was the normal hospitality of an English country house weekend, with (weather permitting) recreational walks, tennis, croquet - golf at the nearby club, that sort of thing. But the secret was in the careful selection of the guests and the opportunity for developing contacts of the right sort.

The sum total of the financial deals that took place on the lawns, or as men walked along the shrubbery paths, was immeasurable. Because of the loyalty their hospitality engendered, Geoffrey and Sonia survived the slump of world markets in the eighties – assisted, of course, by investments in other deals that had come to Geoffrey's ears, as a trusted and generous friend would expect.

Barbara continued, telling Victoria about the distinguished guests and the gifts they brought, especially the Eastern contacts. Geoffrey made a point of reserving one place at each weekend for a foreign customer – not as an incentive, but a reward, and only after contracts had been agreed and signed. The Arab or Asian or Japanese Director would arrive for a weekend of impeccable hospitality and return home with his tales of traditional English country life – feeling that this could be bettered only by contact with Royalty.

Sonia was in her natural social element, and revelled in running the events smoothly and efficiently. Barbara had been drafted in to help one weekend, having in the past assisted with local meetings and proving that her discretion could be relied upon. Barbara found that Sonia's ambition was infectious and, as her eyes opened to a world beyond her limited experience, she determined to make herself readily available and totally indispensable.

"I don't quite understand the timing of all this" Victoria ventured during a pause when Barbara's glass needed a refill.

"It started to develop when they lived at the Manor – Geoffrey's father's house, then he died. It was when they had been married for over twelve years and thinking of moving to Surrey after Geoffrey's father's death that Sonia realised she was pregnant. That caused a gap in the hospitality side of things, so I lost contact, except by letter, for a while. Then after things settled down, Sonia asked me to help with a particularly significant event that involved Governmental dealings, and we have never lost touch since."

"I know she always spoke so highly of you, and said you were her most loyal friend."

To her astonishment, Barbara suddenly lost her poise. Tears welled up and spilled unchecked down her cheeks. Then, even more appallingly, she began to sob – huge heart-wrenching sobs that woke Ben.

"What on earth ..." he mumbled, but a warning glance from Victoria for once stopped him saying anything further. He sank back, listening reluctantly

- totally unprepared for the result of days of tension and grief that had eventually unleashed this deluge of tears and guilt.

"I'm not the person you think I am" Barbara said when her anguish abated slightly. "Oh please let me tell you and get it off my chest, then you can throw me out and I need never come here again."

"But Mummy always said it was your second home." Ben ventured, earning another frown from his wife.

"She wouldn't have said that if she'd known how I have abused her hospitality all these years. I must tell you, so you can decide if I'm fit to attend her funeral."

"Well, *what* happened … ?"

Barbara took a deep breath and began in a low tremulous voice.

"Sonia is – *was* – the dearest friend I ever had. More than she ever knew. We had so much in common – both our fathers leaving home because they had found other women – yes, we shared that disgrace, we found out later. In those days it was a stigma that was impossible to cope with, and Sonia's mother insisted that she had to leave school, in case her friends found out and told *their* mothers – and that was why we never met. I believe she was ill for several months, and avoided being forced to return to school because her age meant she could leave. She went to secretarial college, trained, and became ambitious.

"I'm telling you this because it happened to me too, and it made me hard – very hard. I became single-minded about being independent, and as soon as I could, I left home, determined that no man would ever treat me as my mother had been treated. I was so bitter. No boyfriends – who needed them? Everything I would ever need I would provide for myself, with no obligations. I suppose I was one of the early women's libbers.

"I worked. Every penny I earned I spent on improving my lifestyle, my skills and my knowledge. *I* was not going to stay in a small town, waiting for a 'Mr Right' as the saying went, bringing up babies and waiting for the tell-tale signs that he'd had the best of my life and was now ready to move on to someone younger.

"Sonia's meetings gave me the opportunity to learn about the things that really make the world go round, and how to act the part of sophisticated assistant to the 'nth degree – and I *was* only acting, as I was terrified of men. I became known as the 'English ice-maiden' because I would not yield to the blandishments of the guests, but I eventually learned to enjoy the power that came with that – oh, *how* I enjoyed it! Then one evening I was trapped in a situation I couldn't avoid, with one of their best-known clients – and I was no longer a virgin."

Victoria shuddered, but fascinated, continued to listen, as did Ben – trying to focus through his alcoholic haze.

"He had been very forceful and I had marks to prove it – I realised very quickly that it put me in a winning position. I could have ruined him - I knew Sonia trusted my integrity, and I also knew that he had a reputation to maintain in his own country. So, when he pleaded with me, I threatened to tell Sir Geoffrey, then eventually promised that I would not tell a soul, provided I had significant recompense. Within two days of him returning home I received a handsome gift – a portfolio of shares. No note, no admission – a gentleman's agreement that he trusted me to honour.

"It gave me a great deal to think about. For the first time, I realised I had real power, and that maybe, now that I had nothing to lose and everything to gain, I could turn this episode to my advantage. By the time Sonia moved down to Surrey I had built up a small but very exclusive clientele – only four or five - none of whom knew about each other, and who were all captains of industry willing to pay handsomely for 'quality' time with me.

"Eventually their generous gifts kept me in very pleasant circumstances, but it was all very low profile and intermittent – nevertheless, I made new and even more influential contacts here at the Hall and we would arrange to meet in a discreet hotel some distance away. I was happy with the way I could control these men and their basest feelings, in a way my mother had never been able to do with my father. I had found a *very* satisfactory way of having revenge on the whole of the male population – and although I gave good value for money, I betrayed the true meaning of love. Fortunately, Sonia never found out – never even suspected.

"When I stayed at the Hall, the code of honour (if that's what it should be called when it's betrayal of a friend and trusting employer) meant that I never gave a hint of anything devious, by word or by look, when one of my 'gentlemen' was one of the guests.

"My flat in Chiswick, my porcelain collection, my watercolours, my clothes, to say nothing of my bank account – all have been provided by my disgraceful behaviour to someone who trusted me. Oh Sonia – can you ever forgive me?"

Silence fell, broken only by Barbara's muffled sighs. Such was the effect of her words that the chill the others felt on their souls numbed their thoughts.

It was a miserable journey back to the Afterlife, made with increased foreboding about Sonia's reaction. Her guide began to wonder if he had overdone the shock tactics and muttered a quick prayer under his breath, asking for help in finding the right words when the inevitable attack came. Sonia waited until she was sat once more at her desk.

"Did you take me there deliberately? Knowing that woman would reveal her sordid past?" she eventually said in a strange, taut voice, "What do you make of someone who lives that sort of life? To think that I have left her so much in my Will … all my Dresden collection to add to her own …"

"It is not my place to judge your friend, or anyone else for that matter. I am here to help you see things in their true light and I tried to warn you that it would sometimes involve surprises that you would rather not know."

"But now I *do* know, and you have destroyed a precious memory of someone I believed to be a dear friend."

"She herself has provided the disillusionment, and I would like you to consider the reason why she had to seek revenge all her life. Could it be that like you and your mother she couldn't forgive? Now would you like to be left to your thoughts, or would you prefer to discuss this further?"

"Go away, you cretin! Get back to your garden and do what you're supposed to be doing! I don't need to dwell on this betrayal - how dare you subject me to this kind of humiliation!" Eyes blazing with a white-hot fury, she suddenly thought of a further tactic. "Who is your superior? I shall put in a complaint so that I need never see you again!"

Sonia could not escape the turmoil of her thoughts. She turned to her journal and gazed bleakly at the next page, wondering if her practice of writing would help to ease this particular problem.

Why could I not see what was taking place? Was I too naïve, or too busy? I wonder if Geoffrey knew? All these men and their wives, and from the best families, too – if word had leaked out, we would have been the laughing stock of the county, the business could have been ruined, and it would all have been such a disgrace. I spent my youth trying to escape humiliation and to have it so nearly catch up with me is too awful to contemplate.

I blame Geoffrey for encouraging me to bring Barbara back into our lives. I could so easily have engaged a local girl with a few brains, and trained her exactly as I wished. If I have any control over who I meet in this Afterlife, Barbara is now most definitely not on the list.

To think that poor Benjamin had to hear all that when he is least able to cope with any more shocks just proves that she has no concern for anyone else's finer feelings. As for her plea for forgiveness – that is totally out of the question, from whichever side of the grave you view the situation. Never could I forgive such betrayal, and that is the end of the matter.

Well, Mr Omnipotent Fu, I will persist in my trips back to the Hall in order to show you how my son rallies round, as I am sure he will once this unpleasantness has worn off. The letter I left for him to hand to Jacqueline will give him strength to rise above any petty opinions, safe in the knowledge that the empire founded by his grandfather and developed by the partnership his father and I shared, will help him prosper for the rest of his days.

He will father sons in the future, no doubt, and they in turn will maintain the family name and position.

Mr Fu stood looking over Sonia's shoulder as she was engrossed in her writing, and left, shaking his head sadly. He knew the contents of the letter, as he knew everything that had happened in her life, having spent her lifetime waiting for a call that never came. There *was* no plea for a guardian angel when a soul was housed in a stubborn, arrogant, invincible body such as Lady Sonia.

Inevitably, more storms lay ahead. He penned another memo.

Dear God –
Thank You for Your help with the visit.
I will work on the forgiveness factor, then take her back just once more before the funeral – she needs to see her daughter's reactions to the letter. The effects of that particular time bomb should make her realise what nothing else has done so far.
If she puts in the complaint against me she has threatened, then please take it with a pinch of salt – hopefully by the time it reaches You, we will have resolved the matter.

Yours as ever, devotedly -
Angel Prince/Mr Fu

$\twoheadrightarrow 12 \twoheadleftarrow$

IT HAD BEEN A LOW-KEY New Year as far as the adults were concerned. Tim and Ella had greeted Richard's parents with glee, looking forward to having their undivided attention for a few days.

Jacqui and Richard viewed their journey with mixed feelings as they travelled to the Hall two days before the funeral – Jacqui was hoping her brother would soften towards her when she was on the spot, getting involved with the preparations. He'd had such responsibilities thrust upon him, and although she was sure he would be fine in time, the tension fairly crackled when she telephoned Ben, and meant she had kept the calls brief and practical.

"I'm so glad you've been able to come and give me moral support – I've a feeling I'm going to need it" she said as she realised just how much she had come to rely on Richard. He was always there, with his incredible gift of saying or doing the right thing at just the right moment. He also had the gift of not being too protective, and that was infinitely more precious in a way. Her life had taken some hard twists and turns, and she needed to remind herself that she had fought against many odds in order to retain her independence. A husband, however well-meaning, who took even a fraction of that hard-won strength away would have been doing her no favours.

Richard patted her hand lightly.

"Whatever happens, we're us, and what we have is pretty good. It's the end of an era, and everyone will be getting used to the idea."

"Mmm, just hold my hand when we go through the door, will you? Then I'll be fine."

Annie looked harassed when she welcomed them in, taking their coats.

87

"You're to sleep in your old room Miss Jacqueline, and coffee's just been put in the drawing room. I'll get George to take your things upstairs. Were the roads busy? Now, please excuse me – I'm needed in the kitchen."

In the drawing room, pouring the coffee, they were joined by Vicky, who looked pale and tired.

"I thought I'd better do the honours when I heard your car – no-one else is up this morning. We had a dreadful night last night."

"Isn't she settling well?"

"Oh no – not Lucy! She's as good as gold, Nanny says … No, it was something else, but I can't tell you now … Oh, here's Ben after all – I didn't realise you were awake. Coffee?"

Polite conversation, the traditional refuge of the English in tensely emotional situations, came to their rescue. Richard expressed formal condolences to his brother-in-law, Jacqueline showed sisterly concern at the strain Ben was showing, reminding him they were willing to undertake any tasks that needed doing in the remaining two days before the funeral. Ben explained Barbara's absence by saying she had been overdoing things, but hoped she would be well enough to join them all at dinner that evening.

When Jacqui showed keen interest in the baby, Victoria took the opportunity to take her up to the nursery where Nanny ushered them in.

"Lucinda Sonia Margaret Woolston, this is your Auntie Jacqueline."

Jacqui peeped into the crib and exclaimed with delight, commenting on her looks, her hair and all the tiny details new mothers long to hear. Vicky at last felt she could relax, and happily received the compliments on her baby's behalf. Soon they were exchanging experiences, Jacqui's natural warmth and interest eventually beginning to soften the reserve and defensiveness that Sonia's constant denigrating had built up.

Jacqueline had realised this might be the root of the problem – it was an obvious thing for Sonia to set out to do, to perpetuate her own feelings and create a divide between brother and sister. She was therefore so glad of the opportunity to show she felt only genuine regard for the little family, and hoped this baby would do much to fill the gaps left by her grandmother's death, as time went on.

They eventually retraced their steps downstairs and Ben readily agreed to spend time updating Jacqui after lunch, then she would be able to contact people later. He had found it hard work with only intermittent help from his wife, which was due, of course, to strict orders from Clair the Nanny who was adamant that new mothers had to obey her regime. Although Barbara had been willing to step in - after the previous night's embarrassing episode Ben hoped she would need to spend most of the day resting in her room, until he could face her without disgust. Soon Jacqui was ticking off more items on the main list of things to be done, and prioritising those that remained.

Vicky had wondered whether to say anything about Barbara's disclosure, but eventually decided against the idea, hoping that Jacqui would forget the earlier reference to the disturbed night. She continued to be plagued by thoughts of it – not least because it put her late mother-in-law in a different light entirely. How could that go on for so long, right under that would-be aristocratic nose? Was Barbara being fiercely protective of her friend, or was it to protect her own interests? Whichever had been the case, the result was conspiracy on a remarkable scale.

She glanced at her watch and lay down on top of the bed. Time for the rest that Nanny was insisting she should have each afternoon in order to be able to feed the baby adequately. Ben resented this, as he seemed to resent most things connected with the new regime. Maybe if Lucy *had* been a boy it would be different and Ben would be more pleasant. Well, it was too late for thoughts of 'what if' and she had enough adjustments of her own to make - to motherhood. Her parents would be able to visit when their cruise holiday ended. That would be something to look forward to. Marriage was not turning out to be anything like she had imagined it would be. What would Lucy be like in ten years from now? Would she have to take second place with a younger brother around? These and other random troubled thoughts eventually subsided and Victoria dozed fitfully for an hour.

Barbara heard Annie's discreet tap at the door, murmured "Come in", and looked up ruefully as the tray was set on the table by the window and the curtains partially drawn back.

"Sorry I'm such a pain – these migraines are hell."

So that was to be the official line, thought Annie, knowing Barbara and her habits better than Barbara gave her credit for. In fact Annie suspected many things about Barbara that were unknown to anyone else now that Sir Geoffrey was dead.

"Do you have your tablets handy?"

"Yes, it's easing now. Annie, do you have a moment?"

"Well, yes – what is it?"

"I'd like to think that there will be a chance for me to slip into Guildford tomorrow, to buy a gift for little Lucy, and doing that will lift the gloom a little. Would you be able to come with me?"

Annie felt it would suit her own purposes very well, so she agreed to the trip, if it could take place immediately after breakfast, leaving the rest of the day free to prepare for the following day's event – the funeral.

Barbara felt much better later that afternoon and was so pleased to hear another gentle knock at the door just as she was wondering whether to put in an early appearance downstairs.

"Auntie Babs! Are you feeling better now? I thought you might be ready for another cup of tea."

"Oh, Jacqueline! I am so glad to see you."

They had always had a closeness dating from the intermittent occasions of Jacqui's childhood when Barbara relaxed for a day after the business weekends at the Hall had finished. She had enjoyed the company of the little girl who was so solemn for most of the time, but had the capacity for so much love. This satisfied any latent maternal tendencies that Barbara might have had, for motherhood had never figured in her life plan.

Of course she had been apprehensive about Jacqui's first marriage, but was wise enough to keep her thoughts to herself, so that later, when Jacqui had been having problems with Zak and was being hounded by the press, eager for more of the sordid details she needed, she had been able to give her a place to retreat to, in her flat. Privately, Barbara had thought this was what she should be having from Sonia, but she willingly gave Jacqui whatever she could. Jacqueline had always been less favoured in Sonia's eyes than Ben. No wonder Geoffrey had always tried to make amends – sometimes, Barbara thought, to the point of over-compensating.

They hugged now, relieved to have each other to turn to.

"You are so fortunate to have Richard" Barbara said "I really think he might have been the person to bring you and your mother closer in time. She would listen to him, whereas she was always wary of Anthony. Didn't approve of the hypnosis, she said, but I think she was probably scared."

Jacqui smiled at the thought of her mother being scared of anything or anyone.

"Most of mother's generation don't approve of it. He did sense, though, that she'd hidden so much from her past it had formed a thick layer of control. She felt safe if everything in her life was predictable, and gave short shrift to anyone who stepped out of line."

"Particularly since your father died."

"True. Oh Barbara – I do miss him so much." Jacqui buried her head in her hands.

They both wept - for their memories of a man who, although far from perfect, had meant something special to each of them and both thought of him with fondness and gratitude.

"I wonder if they're together now …" mused Jacqui. "I suppose I shall never find the cause of my mother's dislike, but I do wish them both peace and happiness. Perhaps Mummy will find it in her heart to forgive me for whatever I kept doing wrong. When I was little I always wondered why she treated me so harshly. It wasn't too bad when there were people around – visitors, you know. But when we were alone she ignored me as much as possible, otherwise, something I said or did would work her up into one of those terrible tempers.

"It was awful, and when Daddy was there, somehow it was even worse, although she never let him see her hitting me. She would say the most hurtful things to me and threaten to kill my pets. I could never understand why, and I really did try to be a good girl. Daddy would comfort me afterwards, and spend time with me until he was sure I wasn't upset, but somehow he never seemed able to prevent her punishing me, no matter how unfair it was."

"Barbara held her hand and squeezed it lightly, not interrupting the flow of something that Jacqui obviously needed to talk about.

"When I met Anthony I'd managed to forget a great deal of this. You know how my marriage to Zak, and all that publicity had left me - I was just about holding things together for Timmy's sake. Anthony helped me to start piecing things together, and I learned the reasons for many of my reactions. It explained a great many things that had puzzled me for years – why I felt so much shame when things were so obviously not my fault, for instance. But I never really got to the bottom of why my punishments were always so much more severe than Ben's – much more than you would expect from an ordinary favouritism situation."

Jacqui hung on to Barbara's hand as if she were drowning. Barbara waited patiently.

"The only real clue was found when I went for hypnotherapy with a friend of Anthony's. I was taken back - regressed - to a time when I felt happy. It was a summer holiday when I was about eight or nine. Ben and I were staying with my Aunt and Uncle. It must have been the time when Mummy was ill and we were suddenly sent away. They were so kind to me. I was outside a door, going to the kitchen for a drink, then I heard them talking. They must have thought I was playing outside.

'What can you expect from someone like Sonia, coming from that disgraceful family background? Her father didn't leave home on a whim, you know. He must have had that other woman for years, and his wife never knew.'

"At this point of the session I screamed and became very agitated. The hypnotherapist helped me come round safely, but I couldn't discuss it with him. I just needed to get home, and it was two days before I stopped shaking. I never went again – what other disturbing secrets might come out?

"We eventually pieced it together. They were talking about my mother, and the Grandfather I never knew. I had always been told he was killed in the War, and had built up this idea of a courageous soldier - a strong, upright man who would fight for his country and family. Suddenly I was totally disillusioned, when the memory of what I'd overheard was unearthed.

"Anthony helped me to sort it out as the shock wore off. It *was* a shock, too - instead of a war hero, my Grandfather had suddenly become a disgrace. What must it have done to my mother? Anthony said that a normal reaction would be a desire for my mother to protect herself from any more pain. Her father had betrayed both mother and daughter, so the young Sonia might well think that the best way to deal with life and relationships would be to control everything she could. She even controlled your father by making herself indispensable in his business.

"It seemed to make sense, put like that. My poor mother couldn't handle the pain she had been feeling inside for so many years. The illness she had when I was away for that holiday was never referred to – by anyone – and it was not the sort of thing I could ask her about directly, was it?

"After that, when we returned home, I would hear her sobbing in the night. Night after night it went on. My father's voice would soothe her, and it eventually stopped. She stayed in her room for days on end. I remember she only ever wore long sleeved dresses after that, but I couldn't connect these things at the time. Children were only allowed to see what adults thought they ought to see in those days. We were sent away to school soon afterwards, and that helped me, as it was a means of escaping. It set a pattern, though, and Anthony explained how my first marriage had also been an escape – anything rather than return to that unhappy house.

"Ben coped much better, of course. Mummy was more tranquil when he was with her. It must have been a strain for her, all those years of keeping up pretences, being hostess for all Daddy's business guests. If it hadn't been for you, Barbara, she might never have got through it.

"When Anthony helped me to realise what had been happening, I decided to see if there might be a way I could help her. I kept it low key, of course, but I made sure I was in regularly in touch. It wasn't easy. I know that with my first marriage I'd given her plenty of things in my life to be scathing about, but I couldn't bear malice towards someone who was as sick as she had been.

I clung on to the hope that if I loved her enough it would eventually smooth things out. But then when Daddy died, it made her very bitter."

Barbara had been listening intently as she drank her tea and gradually returned to her normal self. She held Jacqui's hand silently for several more minutes, then gave a reassuring pat.

"Time helps us to see things more in perspective, Jaqui, but try not to let the old hurts get stirred up. Only one more day to go, my dear, then it's the funeral and we can *all* start getting on with the rest of our lives. I'm so glad you're here and I'll be able to help you out tomorrow, I promise, after I've been to buy a gift for Lucy – isn't she sweet? And *that's* a telling remark from a crabby old woman who never had any time for children!"

"Nonsense Auntie Babs – I know you've always had a gift for it and my two adore you - you know that, as will Lucy. They are three very lucky children with a fabulous Auntie. Now I'll wait for you to get ready and we'll go downstairs together."

Jacqueline knew that practicality would be the best antidote to her emotional conversation and busied herself with the remaining phone calls that afternoon, while Richard persuaded Ben to go for a walk around the estate, to 'blow the cobwebs away'. Ben found it was good to have another man to talk with, and the fresh air helped him to think more clearly than he had been doing for some days. They discussed many topics, and even found common interests – anything other than the recent events. The early setting sun lowered itself through the distant trees, and long shadows were cast over the winter fields.

Richard breathed deeply as they walked back up the driveway.

"Running an estate like this must take an enormous amount of time" he commented.

"That's why it's essential that my wife plays her part. If she doesn't recover soon she'll have to start taking the happy pills, or everything will fall apart."

"I'm sure she'll start to feel better after the funeral – it's always like this while you're waiting for that to take place. A sort of limbo, with everything put on hold until the final farewell. Didn't you feel that when your father died?"

"Not at all. Mother held everyone together and ran the whole thing like one of their business weekends, as indeed it almost was – more business contacts here than family. There will be some of those this time, too – the church mob in full force and the Mothers' Union no doubt, then there's the village side - the Women's Institute, the Gardening Society, the Parish Council – there'll be many more people than you saw on her birthday; another excuse for the social climbers to take advantage of who they rub shoulders with. I just want Victoria to do her bit, and do it properly. It's not too much to ask, surely?"

Richard took the question as rhetorical, as they entered the side door and made their way to the drawing room to see how the others were faring.

The evening passed pleasantly enough with the aid of a good meal, and light relief in the form of old family photo albums, and an early night seemed to be the best plan for them all, they agreed.

Apart from Ben, who needed to spend time in the Library.

⤳13⤳

THE NEXT DAY, THE DAY before the funeral, again dawned bright and cold. After a more sociable evening, the emotional pace had changed and tensions returned. Ben and Jacqui were scheduled to spend an hour at the vicarage, going over last minute details of the service. Richard had previously asked Ben if there was a possibility of including the carefully selected quotation Jacqui had made. However, Ben emerged looking very satisfied and relieved, Jacqui tearstained and sad, saying she'd like to walk back to the Hall on her own. When she caught up with Richard she explained.

"He has written the eulogy for mother - no need for anyone else to add anything, so it will all be done with dignity as befits her memory. Mother wouldn't have wanted any of that emotional stuff, he said."

Defeated, Richard busied himself, helping Jacqui with some last minute preparations for the funeral, followed by a stroll together in the grounds before lunch.

"Ben's attitude has begun to puzzle me" she mused. "He seems to have taken everything on board and won't take any advice or even suggestions. He's so ... so ... well, bossy, and that isn't how he's been before."

"Don't forget, he has huge responsibilities now, and your mother was very much a guiding light with all her experience over the years. The way she ran the day-to-day life at the Hall was something he knew he could rely on, so that he could concentrate on the family business – now he knows that Vicky will have to take over that role, and he must be wondering if she will be able to cope with that and the baby as well."

"Doris and Annie don't need much supervision, though. They've been running the show admirably for years, and I'm sure they will give Vicky every assistance they can."

"Well, I'm sure they will offer it. I just hope she has the good sense to accept. She's young, and not used to dealing with staff, so it might appear as if she's treading on their toes. But I'm sure it will all settle down in time."

Walking back to the Hall, Jacqui telephoned the children again. Their chatter about games and feeding ducks in the park near home gave her a warm, comforting sense of the loving family she and Richard had created out of the chaos and grief of her past. Jacqui hoped that Victoria would soon start to experience that glow of achievement once the next few days were over.

Annie had returned after the Guildford trip, more than ready for the cup of tea that Doris was always ready to make in the kitchen.

"Did you see what Barbara has bought Lucy?"

"No – we went our separate ways, then met again later, and it was gift-wrapped. I had to spend ages at the bank, and ... oh, I'll have to tell you later." Annie restrained herself as Victoria appeared at the kitchen door.

"Is there anything I can get for you, Mrs Woolston?"

"Doris - Nanny says that she needs to know if tomorrow will affect her routine."

"All I can say is that I will *try* to make sure that everything goes like clockwork - but as long as she understands that it's buffet for lunch, and dinner will be served half an hour later than usual, then perhaps she can be a little flexible in the circumstances."

Victoria lingered in the doorway.

"It all seems so strange without my mother-in-law. Such a short while ago we were all here seeing how the preparations for her birthday were going ..."

But Doris was not to be drawn into sentimentality, or even any level of conversation, and her tone of voice did not encourage either.

"There's a large portion of that cake left, and I don't know what I should do about it. Wouldn't be seemly to serve it at the wake, I suppose, but it will keep until you can decide. Now will you excuse me – there is a great deal to do to get everything just right."

When Victoria had returned upstairs, Annie looked quizzically at Doris, eyebrows raised.

"I know, I know. But I can't pretend to like the girl, and I don't want her thinking she can make a friend of me, if that's what she was trying to do."

"Maybe it was just loneliness. She doesn't seem to have made any friends at all since coming here, and life can be pretty boring when you have nothing to do."

"She'll soon have more than enough to do when we hand in our notice. I'm just glad I won't be around to see what she makes of it – she'll have Lady Sonia turning in her grave, no doubt. Now help me get lunch ready and we'll have a talk later."

"Oh, Richard, thank goodness we've got a little breathing space" Jacqueline fell back on the bed and held her arms out to her husband, hoping he'd join her.

Later, leaning on one elbow, he turned to study the framed photograph on the mantelpiece, then looked quizzically at his wife.

"That was taken one summer when everything was good, for a change, except for Mummy, who was ill. Ben and I were packed off to various relatives in turn, and we had a lovely week by the sea when all the Aunts, Uncles and cousins met up in a big house they'd rented. We'd have been about 8 years old then, and what I remembered most was the laughter. Everyone seemed to have so much *fun*."

"Poor little girl" he said tenderly.

"I've got over the worst now. It doesn't feel like a knife twisting every time I think of what I put up with, and I've also forgiven myself for not having the guts to stand up and tell her about the hurt. So, there you are – living proof that the therapy worked."

She finished lightly, on a purposefully higher tone of voice than she actually felt, for it did still hurt if the memories caught her unawares.

"Come on, Richard - let's put on a suitable expression and make our way down for a drink before dinner."

It was a tense evening, although the flow of some very good wines helped to ease matters. Until the last few days Benjamin and Richard had been on fairly formal terms, having met only briefly at the register office wedding the year before. Ben had disapproved of his sister's choice of husbands even more than his mother, and it was with reluctance he had attended her third wedding, representing the family. However, the previous day's walk had helped break the ice and he was beginning to accept his third brother-in-law, and realise that this time Jacqui had indeed found the right man.

After the meal drew to a close, Victoria peremptorily told Doris she would not be needed further, then gave Jacqueline a slight frown of impatience as she murmured words of appreciation to offset the somewhat sharp dismissal. Jacqueline had always been quite fond of Doris, and over the years had seen just how devoted to Sonia she had always been, always patient, never objecting to her time being used to the utmost. But at least Sonia always made a point of saying thank you when she dismissed staff for the night. Victoria would have done better to learn the same standard of courtesy, Jacqui thought – no point in setting up unnecessary animosity with either Doris or Annie, or life might rapidly become less pleasant.

They all settled down to coffee and brandies by the log fire, then at a moment when all were apparently individually lost in thought about what the following day would bring, Ben made a sudden announcement;

"Well, I thought we might as well get the sordid details out of the way. I've got a copy of the Will in my desk and I suggest we read it."

"But don't we have to have the Uncles here?" Turning to Richard, Barbara explained that the Uncles were Sonia's cousins, solicitors working in partnership.

"Oh that will take place later for the official reading, and we can keep that very brief. Don't want people hanging about unnecessarily. No, it will be better to get it over and done with now."

He left the room, returning moments later from his office, carrying an envelope.

"Didn't really want the Hollywood suspense treatment with everyone sitting round, and I'm sure there will be no surprises. Let's be dignified about it, I thought, and the Uncles agreed when I phoned them – they're also the other executors, after all - so we get first reading now, and the formal reading will be done in the usual way. Then it's just the straightforward work after that, making sure everything's implemented."

Jacqueline felt slightly uncomfortable, as did Barbara, she was sure. Uneasiness spread through the group, but Ben's determination to do it this way was obvious. He opened the envelope, and began to read.

The Will was the usual format ... their mother was of sound mind etc., then after stating there would be amounts set aside for the executors (Benjamin and the Uncles) to cover expenses, the bequest to Doris was the first item to cause a raised eyebrow from Ben.

"Fifty thousand pounds to Doris Forrester for her loyal service."

He paused. "I personally think that's a bit much. But Mummy always was so generous."

"At the express wish of my late husband, the vintage Bentley is to be given to Robert Higgs, in memory of his role as chauffeur for so many years. If he chooses to sell it back to any member of the family, he must receive a fair price.

"Well, of course we'll offer – I'm sure he'll need the cash at his age – just leave that to me."

"My complete collection of forty-eight Dresden figurines kept in the glass case in the drawing room, is to be passed on to my dear friend Barbara, who has always admired them so much.

Barbara looked unsurprised, as Sonia had made no secret that they were to be hers eventually.

"For my grandchild, the descendant of Benjamin my son, and as yet unborn at the time of making this Will, and to any future grandchildren bearing the name of Woolston, I have set up a sum of £3,000,000 in trust, which will be managed by my son Benjamin, the details of which rest with my lawyers.

Benjamin cleared his throat slightly, and glanced towards his wife at this disclosure assuring the safe future of their child, then resumed ...

"Although neither Timothy nor Ella bear the family name, nevertheless they have been allocated a sum equivalent to ten percent of the Trust i.e. £300,000, which will be theirs when they each reach eighteen years of age. There will be no additional amount for any further children born to Jacqueline."

At the mention of her children's names, Jacqui had stiffened, and as the sentence was completed she stifled a sharp intake of breath. Richard, who had been standing, put down his drink and moved to her side, a reassuring hand on her shoulder. Ben appeared to need to concentrate on the paper in front of him to the exclusion of all else, shifting it slightly, and avoiding lifting his gaze to any of the faces around him. He cleared his throat again and once more resumed.

> *"The remainder of my estate - all businesses, Woolston Hall and all possessions - is bequeathed to my son Benjamin, for his unfailing support throughout my latter years, and in the knowledge that he has found a worthy successor to me in his wife Victoria, to perpetuate the name and continue the Woolston line in the family home."*

The air had become electric. A long pause followed as they each digested the import of the last ten seconds of the reading. Ben eventually went over to the sideboard and poured himself another brandy, returning to the group by the fire. Barbara sat motionless.

Richard tightened his grip until his knuckles whitened, but Jacqueline hardly noticed the force he used. The colour drained from her face, then returned with a quick flush as she turned to look at her brother and saw a fleeting expression of triumph in his eyes.

She looked at his wife - and Victoria, for her part, momentarily bore a look that would have been worthy of her late mother-in-law. Superior smugness and awareness of power had dropped over her face like a mask – a mask that only the *very* wealthy can afford to wear, unafraid of retribution.

Turning back to Jacqui, Ben added "There's another document here, in a sealed envelope addressed directly to you, Jacqueline, and marked 'Private', so you may prefer to read it in your room."

It was a suggestion of dismissal Jacqueline decided to take. She walked out of the library without a word, head held high, and it was left to Richard to take the proffered envelope and follow her upstairs, wondering what more awaited them, but knowing that even if it were the worst disaster in the world he would be at her side to help her in any way possible.

Hands trembling, Jacqueline sat on the bed, looking at the envelope, tears in her eyes. It was indeed marked *'Private'*. Underneath, a phrase was added - *"to be opened only after my death and after my Will has been read."*

"Do you think I will learn now?"

"About your mother's reasons?" Richard asked in their shorthand of shared understanding and closeness. He, most of all, knew how she had constantly wrestled with the demon of her mother's dislike and victimisation, puzzled and hurt. Drawing her close to him, he added

"Whatever we find out, whatever the results are – just remember that we face this together, you and I. You are never going to feel isolated and unloved ever again as long as I draw breath."

The letter was cold and formal.

> To Jacqueline Gray, nee Woolston:
> When you read this letter I will be beyond your reach. Had I been alive and this secret had come to light, no doubt you would have thought of making some sort of pathetic attempt to "understand" me.
> You will have heard the terms of my Will. That should give you understanding enough, and the knowledge that I can affect you even after I have gone gives me some satisfaction.
> The facts are as follows:-
> By the time I was unexpectedly found to be pregnant at the age of 38, it was too late to take medical steps to deal with it. However, I determined to make the best of the situation, and insisted your father and I moved to a home more befitting our ambitions – the Hall. I had been booked into a private nursing home for the birth. Inevitably, Geoffrey was away on one of his business trips, so I dealt with all the arrangements on my own.
> Then, only hours after going through the rigours of giving birth to Benjamin, I had a visit from my husband, who at least had the grace to be very agitated. No wonder. He confessed he had been keeping a mistress, who had died in childbirth only two days before, leaving a surviving daughter he had promised to care for.
> Money always helps to find a solution, and he had already made arrangements for me to leave the nursing home with one child, and arrive at Woolston Hall with two.
> As he had already spread the news to family and friends that I had given birth to twins, I was presented with no choice in the matter. In the meantime, I was to be denied any visitors on the grounds of exhaustion. If I refused to go along with the deception, he would make up some story about postnatal depression, ongoing mental health problems, and he would eventually divorce me. Social ruin loomed,

and he knew me so well – losing face was the one thing I dreaded.

Lying there in the nursing home, I had time to think overnight. Something good had to come out of this appalling mess. Eventually I realised that if I agreed, I could be in control forever and I could make Geoffrey pay for his actions for the rest of his life. More than that, I could and would make sure that he was tortured daily. He would have to see his daughter bear the hatred that I could never publicly inflict upon him.

Life at Woolston Hall was a new beginning. Outwardly I became the mother of twins, in a large house with servants, including a Nanny for the children, so that I soon returned to my usual role. The business weekends continued, with Nanny and her charges accommodated in the Lodge. I could live a life of my own choosing - I only had to mention something I wanted, and Geoffrey would provide it, not daring to oppose me in case I revealed his deception.

But I hated his favouritism of you. Benjamin was an amenable child, but you were different. Not so surprising when one considers the mother you had. You are, however, reasonably intelligent, so I need not go into further detail – you can piece things together for yourself.

Therefore it will not surprise you that I have made my Will as I have – you are no flesh and blood of mine, but have been a daily reminder of a deceptive husband and the result of that immorality. I recommend that you be careful of who else knows the truth – your father took it to his grave. I was tempted to do the same, but in the end decided it should be the only legacy you will receive from me.

Sonia

The letter dropped from Jacqueline's fingers, and momentarily Anthony felt her weight against his shoulder increase. They had been sitting side by side on the bed, and now she turned suddenly to look at him. He felt for her hand, but she pulled away, then gave a short, bitter laugh.

"You haven't married a Woolston, – you've been saddled with a b........"

He covered her lips with his fingers, then recoiled as she bit him and flung herself on the bed hitting at the pillows, her voice rising hysterically with sobs and incoherent words. He held onto her, until her world ceased falling apart.

It could have been an hour, or several, but he continued to hold her, stroke her hair, and tend to the woman he loved going through an agony at which he could only guess. When she had experienced the worst, he raised her tear-drenched face in both of his hands and told her, earnestly,

"Never forget – *you* were conceived in love. You were no resented accident, and your father *proved* that, through all your time together. You've lived through the worst punishment and absolutely nothing now can hurt you as much."

He hushed her until she slept exhaustedly, wrapped in his arms.

⇾14⇽

SONIA'S TIME IN THE AFTERLIFE had paused. Time, in fact, had no meaning there, and in any case, there was no means of measuring its passing. She explored the ceaselessly changing setting in the grounds and enjoyed the scenery, but missed contact with people. Was this all there was to it? This everlasting solitary existence?

Her task of writing continued. Mr Fu also asked her to write about her understanding of the five virtues – goodness, judgement, love, wisdom and truth - and explain how she had attempted to apply these to her life. They would discuss it at length - but he would leave before she could make up her mind whether or not he approved of what she had said – it was very frustrating for someone who had lived in a culture of effort and reward to find that the end never appeared in sight.

She tackled Mr Fu about this, summoning him to appear and explain.

"Dear lady, you *will* be able to move on when you've finished this part of your task. As I explained earlier - *you* have to assess your life and the effects you had on others, in order to see if you have learned the lessons you were set to learn. It's no use expecting me to do the hard work for you!"

"But as I was not aware of the existence of any of these so-called lessons at the time, how could I set out to learn something if I didn't even know what it was?"

"May I remind you again of the simplest message of all?" Mr Fu said, summoning his utmost patience. "The message that love is the key to everything, no matter where you were born, or in what circumstances. You must have heard that as the basis of many sermons over the years.

"I think it's summed up by this quote – *'So many gods, so many creeds, so many paths that wind, while just the art of being kind is all this sad world needs.'*

"Love is kindliness, and Earthly lives can demonstrate that, by treating others as we wish to be treated. Every opportunity that comes along is an opportunity to do that."

"But I still say that too many people would take advantage of the situation. The world would never survive!"

"Not if they were all treating everyone as they wish to be treated themselves."

"No, it would never work. You don't understand civilisation. You are most certainly basing your ideas on some outdated concept of ancient times, when people were simple-minded compared with today's sophisticated outlook."

"That *was* when the world began – but simple-minded? Think of the great civilisations of the past – think of where so-called 'modern' learning has its roots. Egypt, Asia, China, Greece, Peru – think of the scientists, the astronomers, and the medical knowledge that has been learned, lost, and had to be rediscovered later. Thousands of years cannot be dismissed lightly, dear lady."

"Well, if it was so perfect, what happened to end it?"

"People began to forget the true purpose of their existence – that they needed to work together for the benefit of all. Their baser instincts came to the fore and they became greedy and ambitious. For a while it didn't seem to make any difference, so they didn't stop to examine their motives, and the greed continued and increased. Think of the way that all kinds of discoveries eventually began to be used wrongly – to benefit individuals first and foremost, and to gain self-glory – inevitably, corruption was the result. Then mankind lost sight of the lesson of love and kindness."

"So why were there no reminders?"

"Oh but there were. They were brought by the Messengers who were sent to all quarters of the Earth - at various times and as part of all the major faiths. At first there was no need of them, with the whole population working together with mutual respect for each other and their needs, sharing everything. However, whenever corruption has started to get to a dangerous level, many Messengers have been sent. But they have always been seen as threatening the new system, so many of them were banished - or worse - so that the greediness could continue.

"Then the greedy people began to acquire more and more earthly power. Fear replaced love. People did things because they feared the consequences, not because they loved the ones they were doing them for, or superstitiously felt their actions would in some way protect them. As the centuries brought us towards the so-called sophistication of today, the blanket of corruption solidified into ignorance."

Sonia could keep quiet no longer.

"But the churches survived in order to teach people how to behave! That is why religion is so important, and why people like me are needed in order to set others an example of righteous living."

Mr Fu paused for a while before he answered.

"You shared a birthday with one of the greatest Messengers. What happened to Him? He was sacrificed in order to demonstrate who actually held the power. His resurrection was another message - that even death cannot kill the messenger and the truth. The desperate sadness of the human race is that some of them subsequently corrupted that message for their own ends, set up an alternative civilisation and called it religion.

"It became divided and subdivided over the centuries, as people who had glimpses of the real truth struggled to put that message in a more convincing way and relate it to their lives at the time. Ways were devised of proving that love existed. Someone decided that money could be used as proof, so people could give money and not have to actually love their fellow man. They did not even have to see where the money went – not even if it went into the wrong hands, as it often did."

A picture came into Sonia's mind of a cathedral she had once seen on a television programme. Not an inch of its interior was undecorated – gold everywhere, jewels set in crosses, in the crowns on the figures of saints, and on the sumptuously embroidered robes of the priests who conducted the service. The camera panned to the exterior of the building and showed how it was set in the worst of the city's slums, with people in ragged clothes begging for money from the visitors to the church who were coming to donate more money.

She firmly pushed the image away.

"What nonsense! The world is full of feckless individuals who have to be directed by people of my class, in order to make them productive members of society. That is our duty – to save them from themselves. Read my notes again and you will see how the system works."

"I have indeed read your notes again, and I was going to ask you to reconsider them in the light of some of the things we have seen on the visits back to your home. You may have been able to justify everything to your own satisfaction, but I notice that asking for forgiveness has not been part of your understanding."

"*Forgiveness*? Why should I ask to be forgiven? For what? Every good thing that happened to me in life has been as a result of my own determination and single-mindedness. It was *I* who made the good things happen, after that awful start. I am proud of my achievements, and the way I have made the most of my God-given talents."

"But at whose expense? Has your single-mindedness meant that you had the best interest of others at heart at all times? Have you ever overlooked others in the preservation of your own progress?"

He momentarily sent a wordless thought up to God and, receiving a surge of strength back in return, had the courage to continue.

"For example, what happened to your mother, Lady Sonia?"

"How *dare* you attempt to distort things – my mother had everything I could possibly give her, and ended her days in the best nursing home in the county."

Standing and drawing himself to his full height, Mr Fu appeared to increase in stature and suddenly became an impressive figure. Not one to be trifled with, Sonia realised uneasily. He responded sternly.

"Your mother died alone and loveless, knowing only that she had a daughter who was almost always too busy to come to see her. She protected you, though, to the very end - *her* end – telling the staff how proud she was that you had made your way in the world, never revealing how many tears she shed in the prison of her room, nor how every day she hoped you would walk through the door."

He turned on his heel and swiftly left.

Although Sonia was startled, nonetheless she was very, very angry. It could simply not be true. The staff at the nursing home had fussed around her when Sonia returned to thank them personally for the care they had given. One after the other they had all said the same thing – "she was so proud of you."

Was it possible that she had secretly been unhappy? That last visit, on her birthday ... Sonia remembered how she had had to prise her mother's twisted hands from her own as she said goodbye.

"I'm late as it is, Mother. I have to get back to prepare for Geoffrey's business lunch. The staff will take care of your flowers and I've paid for a special cake. I'll be in touch – just let me know if there's anything you need."

"*You* ... Sonia ... *you* ..." the voice quavered and weakened.

"Now don't get sentimental, I can't stand it. Just enjoy your day and look at all your cards. I *must* go."

But that was just the way things had worked out, Sonia told herself. No use wasting time over guilt – she had done more for her mother than many others would have done – no expense spared, and she had always made sure that Jacqueline and Benjamin had written their thankyou letters for those appallingly cheap little gifts their grandmother had insisted on sending them each Christmas and birthday without fail.

No, forgiveness was something that had to be sought only when actions were *unjustifiably* unkind. True, she had resented her mother for a long time – for her weak will and illnesses – but she had amply recompensed her later on. What else was this wretched man going to find in her past?

Sonia looked slightly apprehensive as Mr Fu returned suddenly, muttering under his breath as he bustled in "*...really have to find some way of doing it, Lord – does she actually know what it is?*" and sitting down at her side he leaned forward earnestly.

"Lady Sonia, can you tell me what forgiveness means to you?"

"Weakness! It's the one thing I disagreed with within the church's teachings. I regularly had to take the Vicar to task and remind him that if you lived a blameless life, or set things to rights as soon as you could, you need have no guilt, and therefore no need to ask for forgiveness. Strength of character and beliefs mean that God is always with you, helping you to act correctly at all times."

"It is, if I may say so, a very simplistic way of looking at things. But we won't continue to argue. I think that painful though it's going to be for you, the time is ripe for me to take you back again. You don't seem to have understood the message at all, as yet. You saw what your staff thought of you, you heard how your daughter-in-law referred to you, and as for your son being devoted and loving – well all I can say is that he appears to be almost as selfish and arrogant as his mother!"

Sonia wanted to get away, and half rose from her chair. To her horror, she found her wrist held in a strong grip, while Mr Fu continued.

"There is someone you have intentionally hurt very deeply, very recently. In fact you have hurt and puzzled her all through her life, and what has made it worse is that it was nothing *she* herself had done, but an act of revenge on someone else. In spite of your treatment, she loves you. But your recent action has endangered that – and if she loses her love for you because of what you have told her, she will have a far more difficult life ahead than she deserves. If, however, she can still find it in her heart to forgive you, I ask you to learn from her example. It will make your work here much easier. So much depends on her."

They made the journey - Sonia with a heavy lump in her heart, uncertain of what the outcome would be. She did not want to see Jacqueline, knowing that the letter would have had its full impact. She had known, even as she wrote the letter, the intention was to crush her for ever with a burden of knowledge that could never be told, and destroy the innocent victim of her husband's actions as a last act of revenge. Surely no love could surmount that.

With a start, she realised that it had been personal weakness that led her into the trap of wreaking revenge on an innocent person. Revenge - the very thing that she had been able to discuss dispassionately with Mr Fu, without realising that for a great part of her own life she had been so glaringly guilty. There was no pleasure in this journey to Earth, and Sonia felt an unaccustomed knot of dread tighten in her chest.

They arrived in the bedroom at the Hall, with Mr Fu still holding her wrist. There was no escape. Sonia could never tolerate weeping and emotional outbursts – such weakness – but they saw that Jacqueline had woken from her disturbed sleep to find Richard was still awake, waiting in case she needed him. They were lying in bed, talking through some of the implications of the letter that lay crumpled on the bedside table.

Suddenly Jacqui sat bolt upright, shaking, and drawing up her knees clasped her arms around them, as she used to when she was a child. Sonia steeled herself for the outburst of rage she had intended to provoke, but was totally unprepared for the expression on her daughter's face – she was smiling!

"Richard – I've just realised – she's set me free! All these years I've spent so much time trying to remember something I'd done that was so dreadful it would be the reason for the way she treated me. Now I realise there *was* no reason.

"I was the scapegoat, not the one responsible – all I did was to be there, a daily reminder of my father's unfaithfulness and great love for another woman.

"Oh, *poor* Mummy. I knew she was tormented – her suicide attempts were proof enough of that. If *only* I could tell her that it's all right. I may not be her daughter, but she's the only mother I ever had."

"But it verged on criminal ..." said Richard.

"Yes, it may have done, but Daddy was able to see me, and he loved me so much. I could never have known *that* love if he'd sent me away somewhere else. He must have gone through agonies over the decision, and for the rest of his life."

Now that Jacqueline had found her answer, she gently lay down and snuggled back in Richard's arms, a smile on her lips. To her astonishment, Sonia saw a warm rose pink mist spread across the room from Jacqueline's side of the bed. It enveloped her unseen mother in its depths and she looked at Mr Fu.

"*That*, dear lady, is love and forgiveness."

And they returned.

Sonia was very thoughtful for a long time, and Mr Fu knew that it was wise to let her sort out her own conclusions, waiting to join in conversation, but not until she was ready to communicate. Even her journal lay untouched. Eventually she looked up to find him sitting not far away, studying her intently.

"... after all I did to her ...?"

"Love knows no limitations. Jacqueline has found her answer, her true answer, and it has brought her happiness. Limitations are brought about by narrow mindedness and negative thoughts.

"*You've* been the one who has been limited – by the heavy burden of hatred you carried around, and you've never been able to let go any part of it because you were unable to meet your own father again, forgive him, and set your mind at rest. You and your mother perpetuated the hatred, and neither had the means to see how he could be forgiven."

Sonia thought about this for a while.

"Would it be possible to meet him now that I'm here? He must surely be around somewhere?"

"We have your work to complete before we can even think about things like that, and you must not look on the possibility of that sort of reunion being an incentive – true forgiveness must come from the heart, not the head."

"Do I even know how to forgive?" Sonia looked bleakly at her guide.

"Let the love come through from wherever you have buried it. Don't even worry about what to call it – when you feel the warmth and the one-ness, you will know."

→15←

JACQUELINE AND RICHARD DID NOT go downstairs for breakfast. It had been a long night, but he knew that later on, when Jacqui had half woken again and wept, it was not for herself, but for the waste of all those years when Sonia had tormented her husband by ill-treating his love-child.

Jacqui did not doubt that her father's love for his mistress was great – great enough to make him want to blackmail his wife, but he had done something impulsive that, once set in motion, could not be undone without the destruction of the lives of all concerned. All of them – Sir Geoffrey, Sonia, Jacqueline and Ben were trapped into a lie that could never be told while the originators were alive.

Sonia's bitterness had lasted all her life and she had deliberately, vindictively, planned to play her trump card at the time of her death – not content with writing Jacqueline out of her Will, she had finally revealed the cruel secret of her illegitimate birth and the deception of her parenthood – but only at a time when she knew she herself was unassailable, and in a manner that precluded making amends.

"Will you be able to cope with today, Jacqui? We could go home and everyone would understand if we said you were ill."

"No, I'll be fine. Would you do one thing for me, though? I need you to have a word with Ben. He may feel uncomfortable about the Will, but can you reassure him that it's perfectly all right with me, without telling him anything about Mother's secret, of course – at this stage, anyway. Now is most definitely *not* the time."

Ben and Victoria had not slept well either. The triumph that Vicky felt when she heard that Ben was to inherit everything was the reaction she had told herself she was waiting for. Yet it was a hollow victory. She was beginning to realise that what Sonia had made look simple – the daily running of the Hall, the organisational skills, the expectations of the various strands of village life – were not duties that could simply be taken over and run as smoothly by anyone else, especially by herself. In short, she was beginning to develop a fear of what life might hold from now on.

Ben had stayed downstairs with the decanter until well into the night, and had woken with the consequences of yet another hangover. Victoria was glad of Lucy's needs, so that she could escape into the nursery, where even Ben could not come and throw his weight around – Clair the nanny ruled in there.

She woke him as she was about to leave the bedroom, left him to shower, get dressed and go downstairs alone. At least in this household it was easy to avoid each other, she thought, as she made her way along to the nursery, then later to pick at breakfast.

"I shall be very glad indeed when today is over." Doris stacked the breakfast things in the dishwasher and turned to check that the coffee trolley was prepared.

"What time will Lisa arrive?" asked Annie.

"She's due in half an hour, so I suggest that we have our break before then, because it will be all systems go after that."

They had reason to be satisfied with the smoothness and efficiency of the preparations, and allowed a few minutes to sit down with their usual cups of tea and plate of biscuits.

"We'll have to be careful about when we hand in our notice, Doris, but we mustn't leave it too long. I suggest this evening, after dinner."

"And before he sees off too much of that brandy. He's getting too fond of that, and his mother would most certainly not have approved."

As ever, there was not too much that escaped Doris's notice.

"Miss Jacqueline looks washed out this morning, but calmer, in a way" she continued. "She's such a sweet natured girl, in spite of all the past tragedies she's had – makes you wonder why some people seem to get all the troubles in the world. It always seems to be the good ones, too."

"Perhaps they're the ones best able to deal with them. I do like her husband. He was a tower of strength on Christmas Day – so calm. I'm sure he'll be the same, whatever happens in their lives. They were just made for each other."

Lisa arrived early and Doris ran through the programme with her.

"Everyone attending the funeral who is not family will go straight to the church. There will be some family members arriving here ready for the cortege – they're Lady Sonia's two cousins and their wives. They'll have had a long journey down the motorway, so, as Annie is going to the service to represent the staff, you will greet them and make sure they're made comfortable when they arrive. Drinks to be served for them, or coffee if they prefer, then they'll return for the buffet. That will be served in the dining room, the same as we did on Christmas Day."

Lisa pulled a face.

"I feel that she's around, watching."

"Nonsense! You've been seeing too many late night films, my girl. The only spirits here are in the drinks cabinet, now give me a hand with emptying the dishwasher."

Her matter-of-fact approach gave the girl confidence, as did a motherly hug, and they were soon too engrossed in their work for Lisa to have any further fears.

The small church was filling rapidly, even half an hour before the service was due to begin. People from the village, from the various organisations with which Lady Sonia had been connected nationally and locally, people from the business world – all about to pay their last respects. Conversations in subdued whispers, discreet nods of heads, then a stir of expectancy as the vicar moved down the main aisle with his servers, to meet, turn, and lead the procession to the front of the church.

The coffin was covered with the most magnificent flowers – huge white lilies in profusion with cascades of delicate yellow and cream freesias set against rich dark green foliage. Benjamin and Jacqueline headed the mourners, with Victoria and Richard following, then the Uncles and their wives. Once they had settled in their pews the service began.

Sonia had begged to be allowed to attend her own funeral, and watched entranced and triumphant, Mr Fu at her side, floating near the organ loft. She was gratified by the elaborate display of flowers on her coffin, by the well-rehearsed choir, and by the sight of so many people attending to pay her their last respects. It was a fitting service indeed. The hymns had been chosen well, all of them sung to well-known tunes so that there would be none of the embarrassment of non-regular churchgoers struggling to join in. The lesson, read by Benjamin, included his mother's favourite reference to 'Heaven's many mansions.'

The Vicar began his address.

"It is with gratitude that I receive the honour bestowed upon me by Lady Sonia of conducting this service. She had determined that it should be in this, her local church - yet another demonstration of how she had always remembered her own humble origins. Never too proud to overlook local matters, there are examples of people sitting here who would not be where they are today, were it not for the intervention of her Ladyship ..." his gaze swept seemingly innocuously across the congregation, pausing for a split second as he reached Annie's gaze, Sonia noticed, feeling satisfaction and hoping that Annie would feel ashamed at her loose talk with Doris.

"... and I know it is an old-fashioned expression, but she was a true pillar of the church and all that it stands for."

He had obviously spent a great deal of time ensuring he neglected no-one's connections. He recounted acts of generosity that encompassed everything from the stained glass window installed in memory of her late husband, Sir Geoffrey, and omitted nothing that their benefactor had done for the church and the village. It was a list that sounded worthy of the greatest in the land, and as the Vicar drew it to a close, he exhorted each and every one there present to emulate the woman they had all been privileged to meet or to know.

Jacqueline and Benjamin sat in the family pew with Victoria and Richard. Jacqui held Richard's hand tightly, looking pale and drawn but determined to retain her composure, trying to forget the hollow sound of the Vicar's words now that she knew so much more about her mother. She wanted desperately to hang on to good things to remember, and consoled herself that the public things were true and good, no matter what had happened in Sonia's personal life.

Ben sat with an air of what could only be described as smugness. His position was becoming clearer with every day that passed. Now he was destined to take his place as titular head of the community, Victoria would have to take her share of the burden. She would have to take over the committee work that his mother had done for so many years, and would soon find herself so occupied that she would have no time for moods and sulks. By the time summer came she would no doubt be thriving on it, and why not? She was being provided with a lifestyle that many women would envy, so she had no option but to co-operate. He wondered what exactly had been the contents of his sister's letter – not good, judging by the state she had been in, when she and Richard had appeared, just before the cortege approached the Hall for Sonia's last short journey.

Victoria herself wished she were anywhere but here, sitting on this hard pew, just days after her child had been born. Ben had insisted she attend. She felt nothing but anger towards her late mother-in-law – anger that Sonia had stolen the show in the most appalling way possible at the birthday party; anger that Lucy had been cheated of the attention that should rightfully have been hers at her birth; anger that Sonia had not hung on long enough to allow Victoria to ease herself gently into the new life; anger that Ben held her responsible for his mother's death.

Richard sat beside Jacqui, her cold hand in his, willing her not to give way. She had surely had enough to deal with in the last twenty-four hours, and it was not over yet, but at least she would be spared the formal reading of the Will, having had the preview the night before. However, even that had paled into insignificance alongside the contents of Sonia's letter. He was not surprised by his wife's reaction after the initial shock. Jacqui was always the one who saw under the surface of anyone's actions and her compassion for her mother, after all the years of Sonia's ill-treatment of her, was so typical of the woman he loved. He would do his utmost to make sure that his wife and her children wanted for nothing, and above all, he hoped that one day they would be able to have children of their own. But not yet. Not until this pain had eased out of her life a little.

Also sat in the family pew was Barbara, in deep mourning. Black always became her; she had the complexion for it. Her looks were still striking and reminiscent of her heyday, and there were a few surreptitious glances in her direction, resulting in fingers eased round shirt collars by elderly gentlemen, no doubt with memories of their own to entertain them through the service.

It eventually drew to a close. The family party followed the coffin and bearers out of the church as the organist broke into his rendering of the triumphant 'Zadok the Priest', Sonia's favourite piece of music, and the strains followed them along the pathway to the graveside for the private interment alongside her husband, while the rest of the congregation filed outside and stood talking. The much briefer graveside ceremony was soon over and the mourners returned to make their way to the Hall.

Many of the assembly were there for reasons other than lamenting the late Lady Woolston. Some were blatantly curious to see inside the home of the woman who had run their organisations. They had heard descriptions from a few privileged committee members, but now here was a chance to see for themselves. There was the county set, of course – not friends, naturally, but it had been felt that a token few making an acknowledgement would be appreciated. Businessmen and their dutiful wives attended, either to say farewell to an era or hoping to receive a welcome from the new regime.

Eventually the main party was seen arriving outside the Hall with the Vicar, and a respectful hush greeted them as they entered their large country home. Benjamin and Jacqueline moved among the gathering, shaking hands and murmuring thanks for their condolences.

"I don't know half of these people" Ben had commented to his wife "but it just shows how widely Mummy was respected."

The trays of sherry circulated and when everyone was holding a glass, Ben asked for silence and proposed a toast.

"To Sonia, Lady Woolston, now resting in the peace that is her due."

"Lady Sonia ... to Sonia" echoed around the room.

Sonia, from a high vantage point, could not resist a self-satisfied smirk. It had been a very gratifying funeral, and one that people would talk about for years to come, no doubt. So many of the great and the good in attendance, so many wonderful tales of her life recounted so that all would know what a benefactor had lived in their midst.

But there was more to come – snatches of conversation drifted upwards.

" ... the end of an era, thank goodness ..."
" ... absolutely ruthless in business dealings ..."
" ... *now* we can get on, without her interference ..."
" ... certainly didn't understand democracy ..."
"... those awful meetings when she over-ruled us ..."
" ... she only did it if *she* could benefit ..."

" ... personally, I could never stand her ..."

" ... no *real* breeding, of course ..."

Unable to believe her ears, Sonia dared to look at Mr Fu, who thankfully showed no sign of hearing the appalling comments, and they retreated to the conservatory, where Barbara and Jacqueline were sitting in the heavily scented atmosphere among the lush foliage.

Benjamin had done his duty, and emotion threatened to take over, so he had excused himself for a moment and hastened through the library door. The strain and the alcohol consumption of the last ten days had taken their toll. Victoria saw him disappearing and followed him into the library.

"For heaven's sake, Ben, you have guests to see to. You go on about my responsibilities – what about yours? I'm not going to cover up for your lack of manners – I'm going up to Lucy."

"Oh, no you don't - we pay a huge amount of money to that wretched Nanny so that you *don't* have to see Lucy all the time. Stay here and deal with the guests – *I'll* let you know when it's appropriate to leave."

"I would only be a minute ..."

"No doubt that's what you were saying when you left my mother ill and alone, with no-one to comfort her in her last moments. Don't ever forget that you did that – *I* won't."

So this was the way it was to be - Victoria thought wretchedly - always the danger of being reminded that in Ben's eyes she was responsible for his mother's death. Then, with an effort worthy of her late mother-in-law, she straightened her spine and walked swiftly through to the conservatory, smiling that smile she had learned early on from Sonia – the smile only on the lips, not reaching the eyes and making no direct contact with other people. It bespoke of other things to be done, more pressing needs than those of ordinary mortals, aimed at giving the impression that if one then became the object of her attention, it was an honour bestowed.

Jacqui was there, with an arm around Barbara, who had eventually found the situation very difficult to cope with now that her own secret had been divulged to Ben and Victoria in those unguarded, brandy-fuelled moments. She wished that she'd not said a word and was glad that Jacqui didn't know.

But Victoria, fuelled with malicious spite, came across them, and in her raw state of nerves she had to lash out at someone.

"I'm surprised you don't feel contaminated, Miss Goody-goody Jacqueline - being in the same room as that whore."

Jacqui looked startled, as much by the unprovoked attack as by the actual words.

"Don't tell me you're another one who didn't know – she must have really enjoyed laughing up her sleeve at the lot of you. Providing her services for all those businessmen and making a nice profit, too."

Barbara looked horrified.

"I didn't mean to ..."

"Of *course* you didn't. It just goes to show how stupid Sonia must have been, not noticing what went on under her nose. Maybe she had some appalling secrets herself."

Jacqui thought of the letter and shivered, but leapt to her mother's defence.

"Vicky, *please* ... I don't know what you're talking about, but my mother was a very special person, as you must know from Ben. Any troubles she had were not paraded in public, as above all she had dignity. I intend to do the same and keep her private life private. I'm proud to have been born a Woolston, and all who bear that name, whether by right or by marriage, should respect her memory. We know you're upset as well, but for goodness sake, please try to be kind."

Sonia looked down on the scene. All the scathing comments, the betrayals from people she had known for years, had been sending shock waves through her soul. But the biggest shock was the way Jacqui had, after all the years of being the scapegoat for Sonia's wrath, and within hours of knowing the reason for Sonia's hatred – *Jacqueline*, of all people, had been the one to defend her. It would have been easy for her to divulge her mother's secret, easy to use Victoria to upset Benjamin - but she had kept quiet – even though it meant that she would give up her legal rights as first-born.

Sonia experienced something that felt like a physical thunderbolt. She turned to Mr Fu, her face betraying that the moment of realisation had come.

"Oh, what *have* I done?"

"You were human, dear lady. Come – it is time to return to the Afterlife. Now we can start your work properly."

The last glimpse of her old home was the red winter sun setting over the copse to the West, casting a glow on the frost covered earth. The shadows of bare trees lay long and low across the fields and people were starting to walk to cars parked in the sweep of the drive.

Fortunately, she was spared knowledge of a final secret that would have broken her completely - Mr Fu's intervention had been timely.

⇥16⇤

ANNIE AND DORIS CLEARED THE debris in the kitchen. There was no-one else left in the Hall now apart from Benjamin and Victoria, Nanny and Lucy. Jacqueline and Richard had decided to return home after the scene in the conservatory – she felt she had heard enough for one day, and the Uncles, having decided there was no need for a formal reading, were heading back home, after arranging an appointment at the London office with Ben and his accountant for the following week. Barbara had also decided to depart – to the security of her home in Chiswick where she could phone friends and safely sink into despondency and memories of times past.

"Shall we have ten minutes with a cup of tea?"
Annie settled into her chair by the table as Doris poured their drinks.
"When shall we tell them, then?"
"As soon as possible, I'd say – when we've served dinner and cleared away - then we'll hand in our notice. Did you see how upset Miss Jacqueline was? Couldn't stay for even a minute more and you can't blame her, after the way she's been treated. Very upset, little Lisa was when she overheard what was said in the conservatory by Mrs Woolston. Didn't expect it from posh people, she told me – she could get that sort of thing on the telly."
"Just as well Miss Jacqueline's got that lovely husband to take care of her. You can see he wouldn't let anyone harm her."
"Wish I'd had a man in my life who was like that – I wouldn't be sitting here now if I had."

"I did – for a while. In fact that's what I want to tell you – the full story of how I came here and how I found love. I think you should know now, so that we have no secrets - yet it *is* a risk."

"What on earth do you mean, love?"

"Well I *want* to tell you, but I'm also afraid it will upset our friendship if you see me in a different light."

"Oh, for goodness' sake – I'm not going to fall out with you, whatever it is. You know me – if I don't like something, I'll say so, then it's gone. I don't hold things against people for evermore."

Annie paused, took a deep breath, and gazing into her half empty cup, eventually started.

"I can still never think of Surbiton without a shudder. The assault had been awful, and the Police in those days, unkind and uncaring – no cosy suites for interviewing victims, no sympathy – more of an attitude of 'she must have brought it on herself'. No offer of support - even when it was found that I was one of several women attacked, but the only one prepared to be a witness. Yet it proved to be the making of me in a strange way.

"As you know, I lived at the edge of the village. Just after it happened, even going to the village shop became an ordeal. People would move aside, seemingly not wanting to be contaminated. One or two brave souls would say "good morning" as I passed, but it was hardly meant as a conversation opener. I soon gave up the attempt, lapsed into depression and relied on a weekly trip into Guildford to obtain essentials. For the remainder of the week I hardly ever ventured out, except to the doctor's once a month for my next prescription. I lived day by day and some days the numbing feeling wouldn't arrive until the dose had been doubled.

"My one constant caller was the Vicar's sister. D'you remember her? She was his housekeeper at the Vicarage. Every Tuesday afternoon there would be a knock at the door, and I would hide. A note would be pushed through the letterbox, saying she hoped I was managing and if there was anything she could do in the meantime, I should let her know … then she would call again next week.

"One Tuesday I opened the door, intending to tell her to stop pestering, but somehow I found myself inviting her in and was able to begin to talk about things. A few months later, not long before the court case, I'd managed to become less dependent on the tablets, and to show signs of wanting to return to a more normal life.

"Much later, I learned from Lady Sonia that the vicar had preached to the text of '… *inasmuch as ye do it to the least of my brethren* …' and he delivered a sermon rich in examples of how even the humblest citizen could do things that would surely be recorded ready for the next life, and rewarded in this.

Coincidentally, it was only a day or two before he went for his monthly afternoon tea to Woolston Hall. Also coincidentally, only the previous week he and Lady Sonia had attended a meeting of the School Governors, where they had been forced to discuss what to do about this Miss Annabel Hartley who might feel she was entitled to resume her previous duties in the infants' dinner hall each day.

"Well, we know how her mind would have worked - her interest in me was more for herself, but it would look so generous to any outsider if she took me under her wing. She would certainly have acquired a willing assistant. She knew my background, of course – no family, no ties, rented house, and low paid work at the school, where they didn't want me to remain in contact with little children. Meek, biddable, and above all *grateful* – I would be an ideal person to help in the house. Whether or not this act was recorded in Heaven, it would surely be noted in the village and brought to the attention of the Bishop, no doubt - which would also impress. I'm sorry if I sound cynical, but as the years went on, I could see how she always took advantage of the situation and I had no choice."

She cleared her throat and dabbed her eyes while Doris poured more tea for them both

"I came here as soon as the court case was finished, although my evidence was insufficient and the man walked free with a smirk on his face. I was an object of charity, but to tell you the truth, I didn't much care one way or the other – not even when she said she would change my name from Annabel to Annie – and at least being busy stopped me brooding. I lived in the Lodge and kept it prepared and ready for visitors, as well as doing work over here. As Lady Sonia had intended, I really was eternally grateful and prepared to do anything to demonstrate that gratitude.

"Sir Geoffrey knew who I was, of course, but took little notice. Our paths seldom crossed, with him being away so much. Then about a year after I had moved in, he called at the Lodge one evening to deliver a message from Lady Sonia, intending to carry on for a walk. It was the second anniversary of the actual event, and I was feeling low. I was in tears when I opened the door, so it seemed natural that he offered to comfort me - a friendly arm round my shoulders - that was all."

Annie paused, stirring her tea slowly and wiped a tear with the back of her hand. Doris froze, her own cup halfway to her lips, and looked across enquiringly.

"I know, I know … Oh Doris, he was a real gentleman, and it was just a warm hug that I found comforting. It didn't feel as if he was about to take advantage of me, or anything like that, and I never expected it to be repeated.

But of course, it was, and finding he was welcome, he returned again … and again."

"I *never* guessed, dear. You always were one to keep yourself to yourself, and you both must have been so careful. I can't say I blame Sir Geoffrey, because you were an attractive woman – you still are."

Annie carried on, lost in her own thoughts.

"It went on for years, and it meant so much to me - I really loved him and he knew that. One evening, while Sonia was staying overnight in London on one of her prolonged shopping trips, Geoffrey surprised me by outlining a financial arrangement he'd made for my benefit. 'A secret trust fund' he'd said. 'But if I go first, you won't be able to collect until after Sonia's death, and provided you've not left her. That way *nobody* need ever know - except you, me and the lawyers who've set it up.'

"It kept me tied to Sonia, of course, but that had advantages too. Knowing that my nest egg was safely tucked away and gaining interest has given me a sense of security. I just continued to work and was the soul of discretion at all times. The arrangement continued until Geoffrey became too ill to continue his secret visits. Oh Doris, that was the worst - it was agony to see him when I took up the meal trays and not be able to do anything. He knew how much I loved him, though. It was terrible when he died, but I couldn't show what I felt in case Lady Sonia suspected."

Doris was stunned. She had never suspected anything like that. Indeed, why should she? Annie worked in the Hall, mainly upstairs doing Lady Sonia's bidding, then returning to the Lodge when her duties were finished, keeping herself to herself. The ultimate in discretion indeed, but in a way she was quite glad that there had been something more worthwhile in Annie's life than just the daily round of work. She had known about the attack all those years ago, of course, but that was something that could happen to any woman in an unguarded moment. It had been village gossip, and filtered through to the Hall, then died down. Annie had come to work there later, but Doris had just thought she was very reserved, not realising she had been ill and depressed.

Her friend broke into her thoughts.

"I've been in touch with the lawyers this week now that Lady Sonia's died, and the trust fund has been looked after very well. There's more than I thought possible, so I've decided to take a holiday in Spain and look for a place to buy – would you come with me? Two heads are better than one!"

Doris was startled.

"*Could* we? Go on holiday, I mean? I know there's supposed to be something in the Will for me – Madam referred to it often enough when she wanted me to do extra, but I'm not one to count my chickens ..."

"Don't worry so much – my treat, if you've been left nothing, and we'll go Dutch if you have!"

For the first time in her life Annie understood, and was beginning to enjoy, what was contained in the feeling of power, of being in control, and the freedom it brought. This was what Sonia had known all her life, she mused. Now it was her turn.

"Here's to freedom" she called across the table, raising her cup "and God bless dear Geoffrey for making it possible."

⇥17⇤

SONIA'S WORK CONTINUED WHEN MR FU felt she was ready. He allowed her to overcome the initial shock of what she had seen and overheard at the Hall, although he was careful not to fall into the trap of allowing her to rationalise things to a point of absolving herself from all blame.

But if he had stage-managed the whole event he could not have done better. He sent heartfelt thanks to God. She *had* to see and hear the incontrovertible truth and realise that the image she had of herself had been almost solely in her own mind. Self-delusion is the hardest thing to unravel, he thought, remembering some of his past cases.

His next intervention had to be judged carefully. Too soon, and she would resurrect her anger: not soon enough, and she would have retreated into her armour of denial. He prayed for guidance and was advised to catch her unawares.

The flowers did the trick. Entering her room he stepped forward with the armful of freesias and lilies.

"Oh, my favourites!" she exclaimed, startled, and before she could bite her tongue. She buried her face in their fragrances, yearning to be back in her own home, back in control – anywhere but here.

"Dear Lady Sonia - I know I made it hard for you. It had to happen that way, believe me. We can talk later. But first take your flowers, have some refreshment and let us enjoy each other's company. Then you can spend some time in the Healing Temple and experience what that can do."

It was bewildering. But suddenly it was easier to obey than to argue. Feeling child-like, she saw that delicate china had appeared on the table, accompanied by plates of dainty food, exquisitely presented to entice her appetite.

"I know we don't actually *need* to eat, but sometimes you have to remind yourself that good things are not lost forever. Now, how do you like your tea - Indian or China?"

Sonia could not help it. She laughed. Perhaps more of a damp smile at first, but the sight of the little man seriously waiting, teapot poised in one hand, cup and saucer in the other, was more than she could resist. At first she tried to suppress it, but then yes, she laughed!

They talked of other things. She began to feel more human now than at any other time since she had come into this strange Afterlife. Mr Fu seemed to be a different person. She *could* afford to relax a little now he was less authoritarian. For his part, he began see the social Sonia emerge from under the crusty defence she had worn for so long – the Sonia who had once charmed dinner parties for decades. Aware and adept at selecting just the right anecdotes for the occasion on Earth, she had lost none of her old skills.

She felt safe in pitching the conversation at ecclesiastical events, having noticed that he was not in favour of the stuffier aspects of the church - tales of the village school Nativity plays, the visiting party of evangelical Vicars who danced in the aisles to a Reggae beat, the carol singers who had received too much hospitality too early, falling over each other as they rang the doorbell at the Hall, then couldn't sing a note. Innocuous in their actual content, Sonia added details and subtle hints to the stories with perfect timing. Soon Mr Fu was holding *his* sides and roaring with laughter.

"You look more like Friar Tuck!" Sonia chuckled, delighted by the effect she was having, as she embarked on yet another tale of Parochial scandal.

Eventually, when they had exhausted the dainty sandwiches, featherlight cakes and both pots of tea, they sat looking at each other across the table.

"*Please* tell me what I am doing here." Sonia's voice was lower, more earnest. "Do I really have to go through this? I don't know if I can deal with any more of it. *Is* there more, and can … can you … *please* … help me?"

Mr Fu recognised the moment he had been waiting for.

"There may be a little *more*, but there will be nothing *worse*. Everyone has to be dealt with differently, and I decided that it would be best for you to get the worst over to start with. Now you are more receptive our next task is to look at *why* people around you should have acted in that way, and how it could have been prevented. But be assured, you will be helped at every stage, and the first thing to do is to go to the Healing Temple, where your emotions will be soothed."

Taking Sonia's arm, he led her to a doorway she had never noticed before. It opened into a beautiful wild flower meadow where a gentle rise led to a building of classical proportions and appearance. Mounting the steps that led to the entrance, they walked through from the heat of the day into a cool marble interior. It was vast. Marble pillars reached up to the misty ceiling, and elaborately designed stairways led to upper galleries of book-lined walls, reaching as far as the eye could see. The floor was also cool marble, a checkerboard pattern in darkest and lightest grey. As they entered they could see many figures on couches, surrounded by various other figures in robes.

Mr Fu handed her over to a figure robed in blue, waiting inside. As this being took her hand Sonia felt a warm tingle run through her arm, she was led to a vacant couch and a gesture indicated that she should lie down. The couch proved to be soft and yielding. A pillow was placed under her head, and settling herself comfortably, she attempted to use the 'switch-off' technique that had stood her in good stead whenever she had to face unpleasant medical procedures in her life. This time, however, it didn't succeed - her senses seemed to be heightened, if anything. Yet her body was relaxed and her mind seemed increasingly at ease. Hazily wondering why she felt no actual fear at handing herself over to strangers, she waited, eyes half closed.

Then she found she was rising above the couch, and could look down at her body. Fascinated, she saw several figures move across calmly and efficiently, to position themselves at her head. It was unlike any earthly operating theatre – here, there was just a feeling of calm peacefulness and purpose in which everyone involved was sharing. No spoken instructions were necessary. One figure stepped forward and ran a glowing finger around her skull above her eyebrows. The bone and hair dissolved, revealing a tangled mass of what looked like wires.

From her position above she could feel absolutely no sensation. The team dealt with the mass as she herself had once sorted the tangled threads in her Grandmother's sewing box in her childhood. They were teased out and carefully untangled until they lay on the pillow, softly glowing, pliable and glistening.

When they were all in neat strands, another team moved in. One carried what looked like a blueprint. This had been bought over from the Library shelves, and the new workers referred to it frequently. Gradually the strands were woven together into the most beautiful three-dimensional construction, with subtle changes of colour blending smoothly one into another. It was as exquisite a work of craftsmanship as she had ever beheld. She watched in awe, entranced.

Eventually, all was done. The chart was checked for a final time, the first figure was recalled to restore the skull and hair, and when all was complete

Sonia felt herself gently pulled back from her height above the couch, realigned with her body, then lowered carefully until the two merged perfectly.

Lying there, she found that the only sensation she could experience was one of utter calmness and peace. It was bliss! Thoughts came into her mind and out, like small fluffy clouds across a blue summer's sky, none of them staying long enough to engage her interest completely. A smile played about her lips. She wanted it to last for ever.

As if in a dream, she felt herself raised from the couch and discovered that any movement she made was now somehow smoother and lighter. It felt as if she glided across the marble floor. Approaching the doorway, she saw Mr Fu waiting with a warm smile, hands outstretched. Turning to thank her helpers, she found they had already returned to their next task.

Sitting back at the table, Mr Fu volunteered an explanation.

"What you've just experienced, dear lady, is something that will also help you in the future. The Healing Temple is actually available to all - one of the links between Heaven and Earth, so that even people in their Earthly life can access it, although they have to have help from people who are aware of these things through developing their long memories of times past. When you return to your next Earthly life you'll discover more of these links if you take the opportunity to develop your own awareness. The workers in the Healing Temple are those who have the finest minds and the greatest skills, whether they work on mind or body. The shelves full of books are resources – not only for the types of treatment, but they contain the files, or pattern books, of every soul who has ever lived. The blueprint you saw is part of your individual pattern book. It contains your physical, mental and spiritual health patterns, and it also holds the details of why you made your choice of family and lifestyle."

Sonia looked at him, wonderingly.

"Do you mean that I do actually have choices?"

"There is always a choice, as you will see later on when you decide on the lessons you choose to learn in your next life. You will be given many, many opportunities to learn these lessons – they only stop when you have proved your learning and can move on to the next one. By doing that you will be working your way to eventually becoming a higher soul. As you progress through a lifetime you will have the opportunity to link directly with some of the Upper Realms, such as the Healing Temple.

"We (and by 'we' I mean peoples' guides) can help people come to the Temple, even in their Earthly lives – they just have to be led to the doorway and have their helper wait until the task is done. The only problem for those on Earth seems to be that they find it difficult to understand that they're entitled to ask for help. That was why even here, I had to bring you to a point where *you* voluntarily asked for help - and you did, as you sat there in distress."

Sonia listened intently. She felt that all the years of emotional tensions had been erased. No longer was she looking for the hidden meaning behind every word he uttered, suspiciously wondering what demands would be made on her that would be irksome and unfair. The years of warped and distorted thinking had been cleansed from her mind, and she wanted to learn more.

She had been given the ability to think clearly, and understand how her friend had helped. Her friend? Good gracious! Had she consciously thought of him in that way? But she was now seeing Mr Fu in a new light, and he was indeed friendly and gentle, genuinely caring what happened to her.

"As for your treatment in the Healing Temple, some people describe it as having had a mental Spring-clean. I suggest you go out into the gardens and spend a while enjoying your new outlook on life before we resume our work. You may meet some people who will interest you."

Sonia needed no urging. Feeling light as a feather, she trod down a path that felt cushioned with moss. The colours were even brighter than she had seen them before, and all her senses were fresh and alive. The scents from the flowers mingled as she walked down the pathway towards the edge of the garden. A group of people stood and sat at the bottom of a grassy slope, and as she came nearer she thought she recognised one.

This figure turned ... then ... arms outstretched, came to meet her.

"Gran!" she breathed delightedly.

"Sonia! "

Their embrace brought a feeling she had long forgotten, but now recognised ... it was love. Pure and simple. A love that asked nothing, and needed nothing. It was without past and without future, a coming together in one present moment.

Love.

⇥18↤

Life at the Hall eventually settled down, although Vicky had felt at the time that she would never be able to handle the multiple tasks that each day brought. She had panicked when Doris and Annie's bombshell dropped on the day of the funeral, after dinner. Every time she thought of that dreadful scene she inwardly cringed, knowing that she was at least partially responsible, and that there was truth in most of the things the two had said.

Ben had been apoplectic.

"Of all the ... Annie – you ungrateful woman! After all the things my mother did for you over the years – she must be turning in her grave at this very moment. As for you, Doris, I cannot *begin* to imagine what you're thinking of. What about my wife's needs – who is going to take care of things here?"

"I will, of course, leave you and your solicitors my forwarding address" Doris said with dignity "but I can't stay here any longer. Working for your late mother was often difficult, but nothing compared with what's happening now. I've tried making allowances, but you're both so rude and indifferent I can't take any more and my mind's made up."

"And *I'd* like you to remember that my name is *not* Annie" Annabel interjected "so please make sure you use Annabel from now on. It was your mother who changed it – to keep me in my place, would you believe. There are many things you have no idea about, but Doris and I have reached our limits, and that's why we have both decided to go."

Ben rounded on his wife.

"It's *your* fault – I *knew* it would happen! You've got no idea how to treat servants, or anyone else for that matter. You're just a selfish spoiled little bitch who's good for nothing to me or anyone." He charged out of the room, banging the door, disappearing into the library once more.

"But Doris – couldn't you possibly stay on for a few months?" Vicky pleaded, the humiliation of her husband's critical words far less distressing than her panic at the thought of having to engage someone else at such short notice. "It's much too much for me."

"I'm sure you'll find a solution" Doris replied tartly "as a matter of fact, a few *days* would be too long, Miss, as I would never be able to work for you – at least your mother-in-law tried to be a lady in every sense of the word. You have no idea how to treat people fairly and I'm very sorry that it had to come to this. We'll be leaving in the morning after breakfast."

"But you will forfeit your right to any more pay, and you won't get any references."

"It will be worth every penny, believe me" retorted Annabel "and as for references, I don't think that will be a problem – I've had enough of being a doormat, so I'm never going to work for anyone else again. Fortunately I'm not in a position to need to …"

Doris swiftly interrupted before her friend was goaded into revealing things she would later regret.

"We've got all that packing to do. Let's go or we'll be here all night."

Later, sitting among Annabel's cases in the Lodge, they paused and looked at each other. After all these years of biting their lips to prevent their thoughts escaping, their new powers suddenly struck them.

"We've actually done it! Now, no-one need ever talk to us like that again."

"I shall be glad to leave this place behind" said Annabel "too many memories – time to let it all go and move on. I kept my word to Geoffrey and stayed with Sonia – now it's a new life ahead. Spain beckons, and I think I ought to be able to find something to keep me gainfully occupied. Let's have the holiday first, though, to get over all of this."

Their taxi left the following morning, leaving behind an air of great consternation. But of course, Doris was right – Vicky *was* able to find an agency replacement at short notice, the new housekeeper proved to be adequate for the task of running the domestic side of the Hall, with help from a local girl, and Nanny kept the nursery running smoothly and with a rod of iron, as before.

Ben chose not to take too much notice of the changes. He eventually made his peace with his wife, and a handsome pair of earrings to match her bracelet were received with a semblance of gracious forgiveness, thus establishing a style of exchange that would, over the years ahead, build up into an expensive array in Victoria's jewellery box.

Vicky sighed - she sighed a great deal nowadays, and pouted and sulked. How tiresome of Ben to have to deal with the execution of his mother's Will – at just the time when they should be planning their holiday programme for the next twelve months. Having been cheated of their annual skiing break because of her pregnancy, Vicky felt she was entitled to look forward to a compensatory early Spring visit to golden beaches. Nanny would care for Lucy so they could have a fortnight of peace after all the upheaval over Christmas and the New Year. Looking in the mirror above her dressing table, she saw she was frowning, and applied another streak of night cream on the offending area, massaging it in with fingertip movements, erasing the faint line. She could see the reflection of Ben's back as he undressed in the adjacent dressing room.

"Don't you think you *could* manage to spare a couple of weeks in March? Surely there can't be too much to do if your Uncles help out as they're supposed to?"

"That's the whole point. The last thing I want to do is to leave them with any actual effectiveness. They're better off with no discussion - just sign what I prepare and send it off in all our names to keep the accountants happy that it's all above board. As long as they get their recompense and don't have too much to do, they'll pat me on the back and tell me what a chip off the business-like old block I am."

"But we *always* said we'd go away" Victoria pouted. "I shall be bored to death with just Nanny and the baby rattling around in this house, with you up to your eyes in probate and legalities. Then I suppose you'll need to have another business trip."

"Go to your sister's in Portugal, then, and take Nanny." Ben's exasperation showed in his voice. "How about after your medical check? Get the all clear, and it will be perfect weather for young Lucy in that part of the country. We haven't got any seminars booked. Then you can return here, pick up the threads and it will be 'all systems go' again."

"I'll let you know when I've thought it through" she responded sulkily. Switching off her bedside lamp, she turned her back as Ben came into the room. He tentatively put a hand on her shoulder as he slid into bed, but she produced no response apart from a muttered "Good night", and sighing, he turned away from the communal centre of the bed into what was becoming firmly his solo territory, night after night.

Having made the token gesture, Ben was in fact content to drift off to sleep, letting his mind wander through his list of possible outcomes to his

...other's bequests. Her friend Barbara's revelations had been unexpected, but were of no importance now – as she'd said at the time, those involved were now mostly beyond any possible embarrassment. So the porcelain would be a fitting bequest, would retain the connection between her and the family, and no doubt would return to Woolston when she died – if they offered to forget the whole embarrassing episode and give her the opportunity to be a Godmother for Lucy at her Christening.

The other actual bequest was the car. That had been a surprise, but no doubt had been discussed by his mother and father, before his father's death. He'd had many years of Wilkins' service before he pensioned him off. Well, it would depend on how the offer was put, but really made no difference to the outcome. Wilkins would want the cash, no doubt, to fritter away at the Cross Keys, so all Ben had to do was find out the value of the old car, halve it, then make up some story about how he had already found a buyer who was only prepared to pay this amount. Being a simple soul, Wilkins would accept this, he was sure and Ben would keep the books straight. Old habits die hard and there was no room in Benjamin's business heart for sentimental generosity.

Doris's bequest would be posted on to her, and with no hurry, in the circumstances. She had known about it for a long time – not the actual amount, but at various times in her working life, Sonia had made reference to it, in order to keep her loyalty, no doubt. Strange that his mother hadn't left anything to Annie, but perhaps she felt no obligation towards her after what she saw as her years of charity towards the woman, and in any case Annie had proved that she deserved nothing.

It *was* strange, though - Ben was not usually receptive to other people's moods, but he had noticed a gleam in Annie's eye, and a certain sort of – well, he would call it 'cockiness' in anyone else – in the days after Sonia's death. He had been looking forward to the moment in the library when he had privately told her of her legacy – thinking it would wipe any smirk off her face, to find she had been left nothing - but there was no such effect.

As for his sister ... but Ben did not want to dwell on any serious problem areas at this point, so decided he would defer that topic until the morning. He firmly turned on to his sleeping side and let the effects of the brandy waft him into unconsciousness.

Victoria, on the other hand, was now wide awake, having summoned up the necessary tension to repel any possible advances from her husband, and now finding it difficult to unwind. To make matters worse, for some inexplicable reason she could not rid herself of the recurring nightmares that had started just before the funeral, on the night that Ben had handed over the letter to Jacqueline. They were dreams of drowning and suffocation that would wake her in the night. The apprehension was now as bad as the actual dreaming. Ben's breathing regulated then became deeper, and when she felt it was safe, she succumbed to the temptation of slowly and noiselessly opening the drawer of the bedside table, feeling for the glass of water on the top surface, and swallowing the tablets that she hoped would give her some sleep.

The Uncles, James and John, sat patiently waiting on the large leather sofa in the outer office. Ben's receptionist had supplied very good coffee, and the brothers were content to sit and reminisce discreetly about family events. A phone call had warned of Ben's delay, but eventually he arrived, full of bonhomie and affability, shaking the hand of each in turn.

"Come in, come in. Make yourselves comfortable."

The file was waiting on his desk, copies of the Will inside, which he passed to the Uncles. They took the papers and settled in their chairs, adjusting spectacles and taking pens from pockets – keen to impress, to appear as efficient and prepared as any of the Company legal team that Ben employed.

"As you will see, there has been no alteration since the original date of the document, which is quite recent. My mother was a great believer in regularly revising and updating her Will, and this was done with the Company solicitors as she approached her seventieth birthday."

They read carefully, nonetheless. The sheets of paper represented control of a vast financial empire, in addition to a personal fortune, and the property. They nodded together at the bequest to Doris "such generosity" they muttered, and again at the outlined disposal of the car "a very nice way of doing things".

"You'll buy it back, of course?"

"Oh, of course – apart from anything else it has such sentimental attachments."

"Yes, yes, very right and proper."

Eventually they reached the end of the document. Uncle James cleared his throat.

"Benjamin, old boy, I don't want to pry, but being executors we're in a position, I suppose, to ask questions … John – you've noticed the same thing …"

"Jacqueline."

"Exactly. Now I know she wasn't your mother's favourite, but she's left out completely on a personal level. Surely that's a grave oversight. No pun intended, of course" he added hastily, as he felt a nudge from John.

"There's the trust fund, Uncle James."

"Ah, the trust fund for the children – and with such very clear instructions on how it is to be managed. Well, perhaps it was something to do with the husbands Jacqueline managed to acquire – although I must say this new one struck me as being very pleasant. Still, blood's thicker than water, and who better than her brother to look after her interests. I'm sure you'll see that she's not without some personal mementoes of Sonia. Jewellery or something, no doubt …"

"But even if the new husband doesn't leave her in the lurch, Ben, you will make sure she's not overlooked – now or in the future, won't you? Trusts have to be handled carefully. I do wonder what was in Sonia's mind when she set up something that in effect would reduce the value per capita if Jacqueline increased her family - almost as if she didn't want any heirs unless they carry the name. Silly, really. You can always change a person's name. *That's* been done before, in many industrial families."

"I always said our brother had married a woman of unfathomable depths…."

They lapsed into silence.

Ben, arms resting on the arms of his chair, carefully placed his fingertips together.

"Now can I ask *you* something, Uncles?"

Without waiting for their answer, he carried on.

"I know how much of an onerous task this Executor role can prove to be – particularly with an estate of this size, so I have decided to offer you the services of Gerald French our Company solicitor. He has his own secretary who is the soul of discretion, to take care of all the boring administrative details - writing letters, making phone calls – you know the sort of thing.

"You can be kept up to date by post, instead of having to come here, and you would have nothing more to do than sign the forms. Your rights as Executors wouldn't be affected, of course. So what I wanted to suggest is that you leave it all to me. If that's acceptable, then I'll get you to sign this, as a formality – just to keep French happy."

James and John scarcely hesitated. Relief that they need not take an active part was uppermost in their minds, any reservations about the ethics being overruled by an overwhelming desire to leave their brother's family alone. They had endured Sonia's patronising attitude for years, and felt no real warmth towards her son. As for his wife, they had only been aware of Sonia's favouritism extending to any decision Ben made. Their own wives had only met Victoria twice before, at the wedding, then at the funeral, yet often made comments about her manner – none of them terribly favourable.

Jacqueline was the only ray of hope in the family, they had decided, on the journey to the City office. Now *she* had a spark of Geoffrey in her, they agreed – a little rebellious, to be sure, but that stemmed from an enquiring mind and a reluctance to accept the status quo – that was what had made Geoffrey such a good businessman at the time when taking a fresh look at business techniques was a novelty.

He had taken the family business into places in the world that his father could never have foreseen venturing, and moreover, he had built up respect, even among rivals, for the audacity with which he handled deals. Straightforward transactions were boring, but an element of the unorthodox brought a glint to his eye and a willingness to strike a deal that always seemed to benefit him even more than in the obvious way. Thus it was that when the company prospered in those post-War years, so too did Geoffrey's private fortune, with shares and business opportunities that he encouraged to be part of his way of life. True, not all of the shares proved to be golden eggs, but he had a knack of intuitive response, so that he usually offloaded any doubtful ones before they became an embarrassment, and retained some that proved to be golden indeed.

The Uncles made the journey north together, reassuring themselves and each other that they had done the right thing.

"Far better to do it at this stage. I wouldn't want to cross swords with Benjamin over even the slightest thing."

"No, certainly – he's got a streak of his mother that hates any other point of view. D'you remember when we were on holiday that year ... "

The rest of the journey passed in reminiscences of times past, but not missed.

→19←

A MUCH CALMER SONIA LOOKED up as Mr Fu came into the room where she waited at her desk, not knowing what to expect. Mr Fu knew he could be gentle, with no need for the stern attitude he had used before, now she had seen for herself the repercussions of her life on Earth.

"I'd like you to write a summary of what you have learned from your last visit to Earth. Don't forget – having been to the Healing Temple, there will be no pain associated with this, and in fact you will find your thoughts are crystal clear. Once you've done that, you will find that the next task falls into place."

Immeasurably heartened to hear there would be no painful memories, Sonia started to write, and found that it was indeed so. It was as if she were writing about a character remembered from a film. More than that, she could see what choices had lain open to her in every situation and how, by making the choices she had, she had gone further and further along a track that led to – well, where *did* it lead?

She paused, and a clear picture came into her mind …

It was of a great mountain, the peak of which was hidden in mist and clouds. On the flanks of the mountain were many well-worn tracks, along which people were moving at varying pace. Sometimes the pathways were smooth and wide, sometimes narrow and rocky, and had to be negotiated with care. Partway up the mountain she could see a small but busy town with a vast area of commerce – a marketplace that stretched as far as the eye could see. Some of the paths led straight to it, others went past, then back. As Sonia watched, fascinated, she could see that the marketplace was very appealing to the travellers – some went straight there and were swallowed up immediately, losing sight of their path; others hesitated, then yielded to the temptation of the bright stalls and retraced their steps, until they too were absorbed in their delights.

Suddenly she found herself standing in the heart of the market. Everyone seemed to be shouting. It all merged into a general cacophony – she could hear as many languages used as there were people there. Hundreds were bustling about, and it seemed to have developed into a kind of frenzy – there were even people grabbing what they wanted, snatching it away from those more hesitant. She noticed that the stallholders appeared to be very harsh, ungenerous people who had no time to do anything other than grasp money from the outstretched hands, thrust the goods at them, then turn to the next buyer. A number of steeples and towers rose through the clusters of the stalls, some of which even encroached onto their steps. For a few moments it was fascinating – Sonia could see so many things which would have attracted her in her Earthly life – exquisite paintings and jewellery, rich silks and embroidered satins, but she longed for a peaceful place to sit down and collect her thoughts, and turned her back on it, fighting her way out from the noise, the crowds and the smells.

The vision faded.

For a long time Sonia pondered on what she had seen, then resumed her task with a new energy.

I am ashamed of the things I wrote in this book when I first came here. I don't even want to open those pages. But now I can see how necessary it was for Mr Fu to help me go through all the upsetting visits, even before going to the Healing Temple. I would never have believed that my family and friends would behave like that behind my back, unless I had actually seen for myself.

I have tried to stand back and see why they have behaved in such appalling ways, and the only common thread running through their lives, much as I detest having to admit it, appears to be me …

It's as if they had to develop secret lives in order to escape from me. Was I so very cruel? I had high standards, and I was very critical of anyone whose behaviour did not match those standards, and certainly did not suffer fools gladly. The Church's teachings, as I interpreted them, just confirmed what I thought – and when someone is convinced that they have God on their side it is so easy to become intolerant of others.

I wonder what would have become of Barbara if I actually <u>had</u> found out about her other interests? I would most certainly have ruined her socially, and she would probably have had to return to some obscure little house somewhere. But by doing that, I would have lost a friend whose generosity and loyalty has never been in question in many respects –such as the help she gave to Jacqueline when I wanted nothing to do with her; and the way she has been a tower of strength for Benjamin. Without her, life would have been far more difficult for everyone.

Victoria is completely out of her depth. I'd rashly assumed that I would be around for a long time in order to 'train' her, but really that whole project was a pretence – I didn't intend to let go of the reins at all. I'd manipulated the whole situation so they would marry and I would have a runaround daughter-in-law to carry out my bidding - and of course I justified all this as being something that would benefit Benjamin. I have indeed done her a disservice and there is no way of putting things to rights now – I will just have to trust that she will be able to rise to the occasion.

I can see clearly where I went wrong with Benjamin. I used those children so unfairly. As for what I put Jacqueline through, I shall never be able to think of her childhood years without regret, however distant it seems. My only excuse is that I was so damaged by events in my own life. Worst of all, though, I can see no opportunity for making amends and asking them to understand and forgive me. I am now out of reach. Will there be a way of having a second chance, or does this have to repeat itself generation to generation, for evermore?

Jacqueline showed me what pure forgiveness and love is – it's not just saying you are sorry – it's generosity of a kind that doesn't even recognise revenge.

I can see that Geoffrey was a loyal man, in his own way. He remained steadfast as far as I know – or if he didn't, was at least discreet enough not to let me discover anything else after his affair with Jacqueline's mother ended. I'm now beginning to wonder if I actually drove him to seek it – I was so ambitious that I had little time for him, except as the power behind the throne. Can I now forgive him for the wrong he did? Although really it hardly seems to matter, now that I know what great wrongs we are all capable of in our lives.

But through meeting my Gran in the garden I have now been reminded what it feels like to be loved unconditionally and to love in return. Is it possible to have that feeling with the others I should have loved in that way? Can it be, in spite of what may have happened? Can I hope there may be more meetings? I would really like to meet my parents if I can – will it be allowed, and will they be able to forgive me? I'd risk that, if I could just see them once more.

I'm not sure about Geoffrey at this stage. How could he forgive what I did to his love, and to his daughter? It would be a superhuman task …

Mr Fu intervened at this point, having been keeping a watchful eye from a distance.

"They have been learning about their own lives, don't forget, and there can be no meetings until you have both reached the same point of understanding. This makes sure that even though you've had the most negative relationships with people in your earthly life, they too have been given assistance with understanding theirs. All you have to do is let the love come through from wherever you have buried it. Don't even worry about whether to call it forgiveness or understanding, just let it flow."

Sonia's work continued. Mr Fu frequently accompanied her for walks in the garden, talking as they went, discussing a wide range of matters and always giving Sonia more food for thought. She had at last realised that although other people's points of view did not necessarily match her own, it did not mean that she had to try to win arguments, and that she could in fact reach an amicable conclusion by agreeing to differ. With so many of the topics they aired there was no right or wrong – just differences. When weighing up the alternative plans of action she could have taken in the past, she found that there was no implication of guaranteed results – any course could have led to success or gratification of some sort, or equally, whatever she chose to do would have led to failure. After all, whenever someone else was involved, they too had a choice of reaction.

Sometimes as they walked Sonia thought she caught sight of other people in the distance. Some of them even looked vaguely familiar but faded out of sight as soon as she looked more intently, so she supposed it must have been a trick of the light.

Mr Fu was pleased with the progress she made and felt that soon she would be ready for the next stage, although there were many instances that Sonia remembered each time she started writing, and they had to be recorded and examined.

"Will Daddy have been able to forgive himself?" she asked her guide. "I'm sure that he must have been desperately ashamed, or he would have tried to get in touch after leaving. Maybe he died before he had the chance to track *me* down. What will have happened to him? Will he have been able to reach this stage? How does the system work? Will I *ever* be able to set things right with everyone I have wronged?"

He could see how much these and other questions puzzled her, and sent another memo:

"Dear God —
as You will have noticed, she is progressing very well with the
work. I feel it is time for a large reward, if it can be arranged.
There are so many loose ends to tie up that otherwise we could
be here for Eternity.
Your humble servant and walker of interminable pathways -Fu,
Angel Prince of the East

One day they walked through a different way without noticing the surroundings, until they came to a grassy slope leading down to a small stream among banks of azaleas and rhododendrons where a figure emerged on a path ahead, and sensing a presence ahead, Sonia broke off her conversation and looked up. Hardly able to believe what she saw, a lifetime of waiting dissolved into nothingness as she paused, then ran – yes, ran – to her father; to be swept into his arms and the safety and warmth of the love that she had been without for so long.

Then, miracle upon miracle, there was her mother – fit and well, and happy to embrace both of them, the past just a vague painless memory. And in due course they were joined by so many others – people Sonia had known in her life and left behind; people she had neglected and forgotten; people who had met her only briefly, but who wanted to share their love. It was a joyous happening. Surrounded by friends and acquaintances, old and new, she revelled in the unaccustomed warmth of openness and genuine regard of one person for another.

Then the throng parted slightly as a new figure appeared on the fringe of the group and made his way to the woman who stood happily smiling. He was tall and handsome, the Geoffrey she remembered in her distant dreams, and he was holding out his hand, clasping her to him in an embrace that was at once familiar, yet strange. No hidden agendas this time, no bargaining involved - for either of them. They looked deep into each other's eyes and knew that they would meet again, next time in a situation where they could heal their differences with love and understanding.

Mr Fu discreetly left the scene.

Sonia's next entry in her journal was deeply reflective:

I don't know if I will be able to take the memory of this pure love with me
when I return for my next life. Maybe it's what causes the void that we all seek to

147

fill in our hearts. I have learned so much about life through the process of what people experience as death.

I had begun to look back on my life as a waste, yet there must have been a purpose behind it, in the same way that there will be a purpose to my next Earthly life. Mr Fu says there is always an element in anyone's life of developing characteristics that others need to encounter, in order to promote their own spiritual growth. I realise now that Jacqueline is a prime example of that, and that much as I wish I had not treated her as I did, yet she had chosen that path – as I will have to choose my next path and the lessons I have to achieve in a lifetime.

That will be the next part of my work here. I am, naturally, very apprehensive, but I am sure that I will receive the right guidance from Mr Fu. If only I could take this journal with me when I return to Earth! If only everyone could – it would save so much time! We have to flounder our way through life on Earth, not knowing the purpose of why we are there until it is too late, for some. But again, it must be a matter of choice – we all have opportunities presenting themselves.

If I had one thing I could wish to take with me it would be a memory of the vision of the pathways up the mountain – it seemed to give the key to all understanding of what life is about. What a reminder that would be of how easy it is to become distracted from one's true path.

As I did.

+20+

THE FIRST DILEMMA AFTER THE funeral had been for Jacqueline to decide whether or not to tell Ben about the contents of Sonia's letter. She and Richard returned home and discussed the implications at length, from every possible angle, including the legal one that she would be entitled to challenge the Will, as the elder of Geoffrey's two children.

"I could never do that – it would mean that I would never see Ben again. He would be so hurt, and I certainly don't want to take away their life and everything they live for. It would be a betrayal beyond all reason and I couldn't live with the consequences."

"What about telling him, though? Don't you have to let him know?"

"It would be awful to have any secrets. I think it would be better to have it out in the open, than have him imagining all the wrong things. It's not the sort of thing one does on the phone, so I'll go to see him as soon as I can. Maybe I'll be able to see how things are for them generally, as well - I've been worried about the way he speaks to Vicky, and that's not good. A bit of moral support from her sister-in-law might not go amiss."

"What if he decides to tell her about the letter? Would that be a problem?"

"Oh my love, I want to get rid of any suspicions and secrets. There have been too many of those in the family for years. I've nothing to fear from anyone. It will make me very happy to tell him, that's all – what he chooses to do with the information will be up to him."

Richard breathed a sigh of relief – he wanted Jacqueline to have peace of mind above all.

"You'll never want for a thing if I have my way."

"I'll never want anything other than knowing you are my life" she whispered, as he held her closely to his heart.

149

><

When she travelled back from the Hall on her own a few days later, having seen Ben, she felt lighter and less burdened than at any time she could remember. It had been the right thing to do, although she'd sensed he felt uneasy about the purpose of her visit when he showed her into the Library. She had wanted to prepare him for yet another shock, but there was no preparation possible that she could think of, so once they had sat down and exchanged polite enquiries about health and the baby, she fell silent at his question about the purpose of her visit and handed over Sonia's letter without a word.

He recognised the envelope from the night before the funeral, when he gave it to his sister after reading the Will, and extracted the letter cautiously. He'd wondered at the time whether Jacqui would tell him what it contained, but other events had proved too demanding and he had forgotten to ask about it. If it had crossed his mind later, he supposed it might be some information about a private bequest to his sister that had no place in the Will. As he read the letter, however, Ben felt the blood drain from his face, his mind in turmoil.

His immediate reaction was that the emotional content passed him by – the fact that their father had betrayed their mother in that way did not really register in his consciousness. All he could think of was the possibility that Jacqui, now disclosed as the firstborn, might have an idea of the legal implications that could ruin him, if she chose. He wondered if she realised what power she had – it could mean an end of everything for him and his family, if she decided to contest the Will on those grounds.

He looked up at his sister, to find her watching him apprehensively. She held out her hand without saying anything and they sat for some time, each deep in their thoughts.

"I had a copy made for you to keep" she eventually said, retrieving the letter from his other hand. "And here is a letter I had drawn up by my solicitors stating that I shall never, at *any* time, lay claim to any part of the estate left to you by your mother. They don't know the reason, but hopefully it will reassure you. My children have their trust fund, and Richard will take care of anything else we need. Now, may I see little Lucy before I return home?"

Ben nodded, dumbfounded. His first thoughts were for himself, then for his child and the son he hoped to have at some stage in the future. He had always known Jaqui had a generous nature (and in fact had traded on this more than once as they grew up together) but he was unprepared for this degree of generosity, and knew that were he himself in the same position, he could not have been so altruistic.

The shock of being handed back all he lived for, within minutes of feeling it could be under threat, meant it would be a long time before he managed to think about his father's actions and the effects on his mother. Then, when he did, he sat morosely for some time before carefully filing the letter from Jacqui's solicitors, to be dealt with at the earliest opportunity. A visit to the nursery to see Lucy, and a brief chat with Victoria helped Jacqui feel grounded again.

She had left the Hall with promises to keep in touch, and, true to her word, made a point of phoning Victoria regularly to hear about Lucy's progress. Occasionally she would be able to speak to her brother, and although she sensed it was more difficult for him she knew it was only a matter of time before he could trust that she had meant what she said, and once again relax into the relationship they had before.

Six months later Lucy's Christening was the next occasion when the Hall saw a celebration party, but then it was with Richard and the children, and by then Ben's unease had eventually given way to a realisation that his sister had genuinely turned her back on the family wealth, and was content with her life as a doctor's wife and being as good a mother as she could be for her own children. He telephoned her one night to let her know that he had chosen not to breathe a word of the letter's contents to a soul, and had destroyed his copy. Jacqui breathed a sigh of relief.

The Company solicitor had received Jacqueline's official letter with a mixture of feelings – relief that the Company was safe in one pair of hands, as splitting it would have been a difficult and prolonged business, and regret that her decision would prevent sharing out a significant profit in courtroom fees, spread among his professional contacts.

As Vicky was never told the contents of the letter, she found Jacqui's acceptance of Sonia's bequests an example of extraordinary but very welcome family loyalty that allowed her, as Ben's wife, to occupy and run the Hall as the 'lady' following in her mother-in-law's footsteps. It proved not to be the ecstatically happy experience she had set out to achieve when she determined to marry Ben, but she had plenty of time to herself once she had organised several new staff to take the brunt of the work - although the turnover was frequent, due to her high-handed treatment and inability to respect other people's feelings. She had none of Sonia's knack of enticing staff to stay on, with implied promises of rewards to come, mixed with exquisitely judged comments that brought about a sense of insecurity so that they did not become complacent.

The Christening went well. Just a small family gathering, to which Barbara was invited. This was Jacqueline's suggestion, and it suited Ben's plans of eventually seeing the return of the Dresden collection to its original home. Barbara made a suitably lavish gift of one of the antique porcelain figurines, the sight of which made Victoria shudder when she opened the exquisitely wrapped package, remembering the way in which it had been earned.

Jacqui's life continued to unfold into episodes of peace and fulfilment after she had mourned Sonia's passing, and the waste of so much that could have been better. But she continued to think of her as 'mother' - for that was who she had been for thirty-two years, and she found that the letter had given answers to so much that had puzzled her for a lifetime.

In practical ways too, a door had been opened and eventually she might decide to trace her birth mother if she chose – as Richard said, for medical reasons, if nothing more.

Time also passed at the Hall, and as she grew older Lucy started showing unmistakable signs of inheriting something of her father's stubbornness and her mother's tendency to sulk if she did not get her own way. Nanny left, exasperated by the way Ben reinforced his daughter's behaviour by denying her nothing and contradicting anyone who tried to discipline her. A succession of au pairs took her place, none of them lasting long enough to form any bond with their wayward charge, and Lucy rapidly learned that when she grew bored, she could mischievously tell her father tales of their wrongdoing – real or imaginary, and they would disappear in favour of another one who would try to ingratiate themselves with her.

By the time Lucy was three years old she had learned to be a manipulative, spiteful little bully, with a range of tactics employed to get her own way if she was thwarted by anyone, including a smile that switched on briefly when she was successful – although it never reached her eyes.

⇥21⇤

SONIA HAD FELT NOTHING BUT peace as she walked into her husband's arms in the garden. It had been the only meeting, but the only one necessary for peace of mind. Whatever difficulties and estrangements they'd had over the years completely evaporated, and they were simply two souls joined together in the unblemished love that each soul has for another in the Afterlife and the realms beyond.

"Why is this so different from Earthly love?" she asked Mr Fu as they sat discussing these matters, and others that would help to prepare her for the choices she would make.

"When souls return for another life on Earth, they carry with them memories of the life here, which is the purest feeling that it is possible to have. But these memories rapidly fade from consciousness the moment they are born, and so-called civilisation teaches people to accept less than the purest form of love. People are deceived into confusing gratification with love. But if they *do* meet another soul with whom they have shared time in these realms, then they feel a special bond, and try to recreate that feeling."

"I never felt that with Geoffrey in my Earthly life."

"No – you were a new soul in each other's lives. Next time you will recognise each other at the deep level you have experienced here, and events will probably prove happier than in the life you have recently left."

"I always dismissed the thought of 'soulmates' as Jacqueline used to refer to it, along with all her other nonsense."

"The term has been subjected to over-use and has therefore become another cliché – but one of our discussions was about the way that clichés contain the greatest truths. That may be one of the facts you rediscover when you return for your next life."

"Do I have to go back? Why can't I stay? It was all so difficult and unrewarding, even though I had great riches – it felt bleak and empty for so much of the time, although I kept busy with charity work. Surely I have done enough?"

"You have to have many lifetimes, in order to learn the lessons your soul needs. The quicker you learn, the easier it will be to choose the lessons for your next life. We are approaching the time when you can select those. Once you have done that, you will be able to choose what setting you need."

"What do you mean by 'setting'? Do *you* help me?"

"The family you choose to be born into. You make that choice, with the help of the patternmakers – I can only advise, not predict. Now I suggest that you spend time with all the people that you wish to meet here. Listen carefully to their wisdom and love, for although they have moved on into their next lives, they are able to return here while they sleep, in order to communicate with you and others. In their human life they may remember it as a dream, and it makes the bonds stronger."

Sonia thought her head would overflow with all these strange ideas. It all seemed to imply that souls could pass between the two worlds of Earthly life and the Afterlife. She had heard Jacqueline refer to concepts like the Higher Consciousness, but had dismissed it as nonsense – now she was not quite so sure. If she suspended her disbelief, then it might make sense that just as a soul could return to Earth (as she had done herself, to witness the outcome of her passing), so surely could a soul on Earth visit the Afterlife. Sleep would be the most natural way, so that anything unusual could be explained by human dreams. The more she thought of these things, the more she felt that her daughter's ideas might hold some truth.

After the meeting with Geoffrey had proved to be such a positive experience, Sonia did as Mr Fu had suggested, and spent time wandering around the gardens of her Afterlife. As if they had been waiting for the right moment, many people came to greet her – some she had forgotten, some she vaguely remembered: some she would have (in her Earthly life, at least) preferred not to see again. But they all came in the spirit of loving, with not a single comment of recrimination or spite – in fact many of them thanked her for her contribution to their own personal lessons that had led to the development of their souls. It was as if their message was that the harder one's life had been on Earth, the more likely it was that it proved easier to identify one's necessary lessons.

Now Sonia began to wonder about the element of worldly wealth in her own, and a phrase about a 'rich man finding it as difficult to get into heaven as for a camel to pass through the eye of a needle' came back into her mind. It made her own values questionable – she had started her life in happiness and comfort, but with no great riches. Suffering emotional hardship, she had turned her back on her feelings and determined that financial comfort would provide a cushion for the rest of her days - no matter that it was gained at the expense of other people's emotions. She could now see how it had stunted her own spiritual growth. She had even mistaken religion for spirituality, and had allied herself to a way of achieving status and power that had nothing to do with the teachings she had professed to believe.

Discussing this with Mr Fu at length, Sonia wondered how she could avoid the mistake of confusing things again in her next life. Would she have to pass some sort of test to prove that she had learned the value of emotional riches? What sort of family could she be born into that would provide the background she needed?

"You might want to choose a parent who had also had the same or better start as yourself in terms of Earthly wealth – but who had a more difficult time emotionally. Someone, though, who has managed to see beyond it and who never loses sight of the need for love being at the root of all things. An older soul who was perhaps sent to lead the way."

Sonia suddenly had a flash of insight – *someone like Jacqueline*! She saw Jacqueline's childish puzzlement at yet another episode of her mother's unfair behaviour, rationalised into 'Mummy's poorly again', as she explained to her dolls; Jacqueline, reading the letter, feeling overwhelming sadness not anger; Jacqueline, on the day of the funeral, defending her mother's memory. What she had thought of as Jacqueline's weakness and sentimentality was a persistent attempt to use love to help overcome her mother's unkindness.

Jacqueline's bond with her father could have been even more significant than a blood tie – they had definitely had something very special – could they have both been 'old souls', brought together to offset her own behaviour and give each other much-needed support, remembering at some deep level the quality of love in the Afterlife, and recreating it as far as they were able?

She looked at Mr Fu carefully.

"Will I be able to meet people in my next life that I knew in the last one? Do I get a chance to set matters right?"

"It's possible, yes, but don't forget that you won't consciously remember why you're there – you have to work continually through your life, gaining insights and piecing it together for yourself. Sometimes souls choose the most difficult settings to work in because the lessons are more obvious. They may choose brief lives just for a single lesson, at other times they choose a longer earth life so that many lessons may be learned. Or, when the lesson is about selfishness and possession they have to learn how to love and let go – that might happen when someone special is snatched away from them just at the peak of happiness."

"Jacqueline said exactly that when her second husband died in the car crash. She said it was the only way to 'move on', as she put it. Strange how I dismissed all her thoughts as nonsense at the time and now they fit into place."

"Anthony had come into her life to bring her greater understanding, and when he achieved this he left, for he had his own development to work on. They will keep meeting in other Earth lives, because they work so well together. Not always as husband and wife, of course, sometimes as mother and child, or teacher and pupil. When they meet, they will know of their past only at soul level, or what some people refer to as 'Higher Consciousness'. That always brings an echo of the peace and love you have felt here, dear lady. Now, shall we continue to weigh up *your* choice of lessons and family? Then we will visit the Patternmakers."

Sonia wanted to choose as many aims as possible, but Mr Fu persuaded her that two main ones at the most would be sufficient for one life at this point in her soul's development.

"There is no hurry!" he smiled. "Don't forget that many of the lessons will be part of your Earthly training and education – from the family values that you are given from the start, and the circumstances and choices you make at every stage of your life – they are the constants of patience and tolerance. But if, for example, you choose the lesson of material possessions, you will be asked to spend part of your life proving that they are not important - whatever the circumstances into which you were born. Your achievement will be measured by the way you react – with bitterness or welcoming the chance to learn more about life."

This prompted Sonia to remember a business couple that she and Geoffrey had known. The husband's bankruptcy had been a social disgrace, and they had never been invited to the Hall again. But, supported by his wife, it led him to a new career in caring for others and they had found happiness in their more modest lives.

Could she herself imagine coping with that sort of lesson? The new self that she had become after her visit to the Healing Temple felt that she could indeed. It would be a good contrast to her recent life when possessions and status had mattered to the exclusion of everything else. She remembered that couple again, and the way she had ostracised them, immediately cutting off any contact, lest it should damage Geoffrey's own reputation, and, as she remembered, it brought back the feelings that she had felt when she had been shunned by her school.

That was definitely a lesson she had not learned, or she would have been more sympathetic to the businessman friend. She determined that somehow in her next life she would find a way of spreading understanding and forgiveness. Parents who already had those values would help her along the way, she assumed.

Mr Fu broke into her thoughts.

"The law of adversity applies, don't forget, with all the lessons, especially emotional ones. An infant who is singled out for being neglected in some way is often on Earth for the purpose of learning about the true value of love. No matter how affluent their background, their search for love can be long and hard, but when they do find it, it's more rewarding than anything else. This may be a lesson you choose to learn, dear lady, because you spent most of your last life behind barriers you erected against love in your life. If you start the new life unloved for some reason, your quest will be more compelling, but it will certainly be more difficult for you as an Earthly person."

For no apparent reason, Sonia immediately thought of the scene at the hospital she had witnessed, and Ben's anger at Lucy not being the son he had expected. No doubt he had made recompense many times over, but had the wave of disappointment been noticed by that sensitive new-born soul?

Sonia felt she would never be ready for her decision. The more she thought, the more confused she felt she became. But, eventually settling for the aim of learning that materialism is not important, she had to trust that she would be put into a life where that lesson could be learned, and hope that she would be given a personality that would help her learn wisely and well. As for her chosen emotional task of being in a family where she could demonstrate the healing quality of love above every other thing, she was baffled. She wondered if Mr Fu would allow her to see one or two families who were planning to have a new baby, in the hope that this would help her to choose, using last-minute intuition.

Still maintaining her habit of walking in the gardens, sorting out her thoughts, one day a thought presented itself so suddenly it felt like a lightning bolt. Sonia rushed back to the familiar room and found Mr Fu sitting waiting.

"I know what would be the ideal situation and not only could I learn those lessons, but it would be the most direct and obvious way of making amends for my life!"

Mr Fu did not need her to spell it out, but wanted reassurance that she had seen all the dangers as well as the benefits of such a choice. He carefully listened to her detailed description of how, if she were born into either family, it would provide the direct involvement that meant her lesson could be learned. It would also provide the possibility of a wise soul learning the other lesson from observation at close quarters.

"Well ... it's very irregular, dear lady, but I'll intercede on your behalf and see if it's possible."

The memo he sent to God was as persuasive as he had ever dared to be:

> *Dear Lord,*
> *I have a somewhat unusual request to make.*
> *Sonia has decided on a difficult path, and is determined to learn lessons that normally I would try to keep for more advanced souls. However, I feel she could do it - provided she has the right people in her life to help.*
> *The problem is, she wants to return to the same family, and I can see that she has a point, but I know it's not usually done.*

As it is beyond me to see the whole of the implications, however,
I humbly hand the matter to You and will wait for your wisdom
to enlighten me.
I remain as ever,
always your devoted
Angel Prince of the East
Master of the Higher Realms
(Mr Fu)

<h1 style="text-align:center">→22←</h1>

THE BUSINESS WENT WELL FOR Ben, but Victoria eventually insisted that there was to be no attempt to recreate the hospitality that his mother had delivered. Her natural apathy to duty came to the fore and she did everything she could to ensure that her life was one of self-indulgence and freedom, with duties parcelled out to staff as much as possible. Ben's love for her began to falter and he was not averse to looking further afield for entertainment and consolation, although he was still insistent that a son and heir would bring fulfilment to them both.

Vicky's phone call to Jacqueline one evening was to impart the news that she was pregnant again – at last.

"I don't know how I'll cope with two – Lucy's going to be four when it's born and she's already such a handful, thanks to all those useless au pairs. Then there's the morning sickness – it's started already, even though I'm barely six weeks. And of course it's due in March – just the worst time of year for affecting our holidays."

Jacqui listened with interest. Poor Vicky – one day she might realise that it was her own attitude that made life hard, and by no stretch of the imagination was it the circumstances. She congratulated her, then added

"Actually, *I* was going to ring *you*" she said happily "To tell you that *we're* going to have an addition to the family here!"

They excitedly exchanged dates and details – realising they could actually produce cousins within a few days of each other. As far as Victoria was concerned, Jacqui was reassuring and helpful, and she soon felt that she would be able to manage things well enough. However, again she adamantly refused to be told whether the baby would be boy or girl, no matter how Ben tried to persuade her when she went for monitoring scans. It gave her some sort of power to be able to keep him wondering – even for a few months

163

– and being more pleasant towards her. Knowing that there was no element of responsibility on her part for the baby's gender did not ease her fears about how Ben would unjustly blame her if it proved to be another girl.

Jacqui had her own personal fears, but kept them secret, and only to be shared with Richard. From the earliest suspicion of pregnancy she had needed his reassurance.

"I simply can't get it out of my head that there will be difficulties with this one. Call it a mother's intuition, but we *will* be able to have all the tests, won't we?"

"Tests, insurance – anything you wish. But one thing I know is that our baby will be the perfect one for us, whatever he or she is like."

But Jacqui's pregnancy went well, in spite of her initial nagging doubts, and when the tests and scans showed that she was carrying a single normal baby, her mind was eventually eased and she thoroughly enjoyed the preparations, getting Tim and Ella to help with choosing how to arrange the room that was to be a nursery, as well as clothes and little toys.

By contrast, Lucy proved to be a worry for Victoria, and even her father noticed her stubbornness and wished that the matter had not been raised so soon.

"Don't *want* a baby brother!" she would shriek when they attempted to divert her from inflicting permanent damage to the walls as she rode her tricycle around corridors in the Hall.

"It might be a baby sister for you to play with" her mother cajoled, risking Ben's displeasure, as he once again planned for the boy he felt would be inevitable this time.

Increasingly he put Victoria under pressure to accept prior knowledge of whether the baby was a boy or not, but Ben could not persuade her, even when he went on a prolonged business trip in a fit of sulks, with Lucy's screams of anger ringing in his ears.

"Don't *want* a sister! Want a *puppy*! Want a *pony*! I *hate* babies!"

Vicky tried to console herself with the thought that when the time came, Lucy would change her mind – at present the last thing the Hall needed as well as a stubborn almost four year old, was a puppy.

Yet what did her father arrive with on Christmas Eve? Of course – an adorable golden Labrador pup.

"For my little princess – happy birthday for tomorrow."

Later, when puppy and Lucy had eventually fallen exhausted in a heap together in the playroom, Victoria rounded on her husband.

"You are the most thoughtless, underhand, arrogant person I have ever met – apart from your mother. Anything to prove that life is to be lived according to your rules and your rules only. How am I going to manage to deal with a puppy I don't even want, and that Lucy will grow tired of in a few weeks if not days? Are *you* going to take it walks and feed it and clean up after it?"

"No and neither are you, you silly bitch – throw enough money at a problem and it usually goes away. I provide you with staff – get them to clean up. Get a girl from the village to be a puppy nanny! For heaven's sake let your daughter have something she can love – there's precious little of that in this house nowadays."

Victoria fled from the room, sobbing uncontrollably. Life was getting unbearable and she phoned Jacqui for consolation. How was she going to manage the last three months before the birth? How would life be if she had another daughter when Ben had set his heart on a boy? How had she ever been such a fool as to marry the self-centred loathsome pig in the first place?

Jacqueline soothed and comforted, promising that they would have time together when she and her family came for their traditional Christmas visit the following day.

"Wait until Lucy sees her present from Tim and Ella. If she loses interest in the puppy after a while then it can be found a new home – I'm sure you could find someone in the village who would be delighted with a pedigree pooch."

"Oh Jacqui – you're always the voice of reason and commonsense. Why can't I be like you, so calm and happy? How is it you've found the solution to life and I'm still looking?"

"Hold on there! I don't pretend I've found any answers at all. I just hang onto the thought that nothing lasts for ever, whether it's good or bad, so we need to make the most of the good and look for solutions for the other."

Eventually calming down, Vicky went off to make the final preparations for Lucy's birthday morning that also saw the traditional Christmas celebrations. The Hall looked splendid, with the tree, as ever, in the far corner of the drawing room, festooned with the decorations that Sonia had purchased over the years.

"Oh Sonia, where are you now? Ben still needs you, you know – I'm not good enough for him in so many ways. If you're somewhere where it will do any good, just have a word on my behalf and let me have a son this time."

Then, shaking her head at her own stupid superstition, she switched off the light and went to retrieve the puppy from her daughter's bedroom.

⇢23⇠

MR FU HAD RECEIVED HIS reply, and to his surprise, God agreed. Sonia had deliberated for so long that at last she reached a point of total confusion. The choice of family was all-important, she knew, for her lesson of material importance, coupled with the task of healing with love. An angel messenger arrived with two scrolls, which were shown to Mr Fu. He was very solemn as her studied the contents, knowing the responsibility that lay with Sonia's choice.

"Your unusual request has been granted" he announced as she returned from the gardens "but I am not allowed to show you the details of these files. I can tell you which are the two families concerned – you do have the option of being born to Benjamin and Victoria, or to Jacqueline and Richard."

Sonia looked pleased, yet apprehensive at the same time, as well she might, her guardian thought.

He continued.

"While you have been away, parts of your family have become more divided and there has to be another soul element within the equation. Both Jacqueline and Victoria will be expecting babies at around the same time."

He could not tell her the detail of this next life – that Jacqueline's child would have disabilities, but would be surrounded by love and the restrictions would be physical, not mental or emotional, while Benjamin's child would have a materially comfortable life with many opportunities to develop through emotional adversity.

"I can tell you that one of the lives will be brief, but I cannot tell you which one that will be.

Now you may choose which child receives your soul."

Sonia was stunned. Responsibility and opportunity weighed heavily on her shoulders.

"Will you continue to be my guardian angel?" she asked.

"Of course. I will always be watching over you, helping you. You may learn as you get older that there will be a special signal I use when I approve of life choices you make."

"What do you mean?"

"Have you ever heard people talk of a 'gut reaction'? Or sometimes refer to a prickle at the back of their neck?"

Sonia nodded.

"Those are signs that you learn to recognise. Other, external signs can be given – natural sights, such as rainbows; animals or birds unexpectedly looking you straight in the eye - your duty is to be watchful and learn to recognise them. I will make sure they keep coming to your attention – that's part of my job. There is also one other sign that I will tell you just before you leave."

Sonia made her choice, helped by the reassurance that she would always be watched over by Mr Fu. He took her arm for the last time as they made their way to the Patternmakers, and as they paused at the threshold he gave his last and most valuable piece of information.

"You will recognise me by my smile – no matter who is wearing it at the time."

That enigmatic remark was to be trusted, Sonia knew. She turned to give him a smile of her own, and heartfelt thanks – but he was no longer at her side, although she knew that he would never leave her.

Holding her head high, she walked through celestial portals for this last preparation, and into the Hall of the Patternmakers where her own particular tapestry was being designed. It consisted of colours and designs that she had never seen in her last Earth life. Some were bright and glowing, others were sombre and dull. Parts of the design had them mingled in equal parts, and Sonia could almost taste the bitter-sweetness that lay ahead, but the overall impression was that the brightness predominated.

Suddenly she felt herself surrounded, and part of, a swirling mass of brilliantly coloured strands, but whether they were made of light or some material she could not quite tell. Whichever way she looked, Sonia saw intricate patterns being woven – but there was no beginning and no end of the multi-dimensional work. Workers in robes threaded their way through the mass; others, with books, entered notes for the Healing Temple Library. Methodical, yet exciting and challenging, was the impression given to the wondering spirit, waiting to be allocated her unique contribution to the rich tapestry of Life.

Sonia wished she could have said goodbye to Mr Fu. She believed him when he told her that he would be there on her return after the next Earth life, and she hoped he was right – she had grown fond of the little man who had been the least likely person to guide her through her discoveries. She also hoped that whatever her next life held, she would be able to remember to turn to her own guide, knowing that his wisdom was always there to help her through the difficult times. As she waited for her part of the pattern to be made clear to her, Sonia thought she caught a glimpse of another familiar figure, also waiting. Geoffrey? It could have been, but it may have been a trick of the light.

Helpers darted around, putting the final touches here and there, with Sonia standing waiting with a keen anticipation and barely suppressed excitement. She was shown to a couch, somewhat similar to the one in the Healing Temple.

A shimmering piece of the work detached itself and floated towards Sonia, light as gossamer. The Pattern – *her* pattern, her *life* - floated above her, held by unseen hands. She felt it enter her heart and become part of her knowledge. For a brief moment she felt a surge of energy as the realignment took place and then she was ready. Equipped for her new place on Earth, she was helped to her feet and walked out into the celestial light to begin the journey.

It felt strange to be travelling again, and she had forgotten how the pull of the earth made her feel slightly queasy as she saw it getting nearer.

As she travelled she remembered how she had hesitated for a long time, weighing up the pros and cons of each family – Jacqueline's and Richard's, Ben's and Victoria's – one with all the worldly advantages possible but a coldness in the quality of life, and the other with so much warmth and love.

Which one would be brief? Mr Fu could not divulge that information, so in the end she made a choice with her heart, and once committed, she was convinced that her decision was the only one she *could* have made - it was to choose the life that would give the most opportunities to make as many amends as possible for her last one, no matter how difficult it might be.

Already her detailed recollection of the Afterlife was fading. Now she was becoming pure spirit, directed by the power of her own choice - a new earthling that would begin to receive impressions of the experiences of life in the womb, followed by the strains of birth and the struggle that surrounds the first breath. Leaving the intensely beautiful celestial light behind, she aligned, and waited for nine months.

Early in the following Spring, after the soothing comfort of the womb, there would be the harsh lights and loud noises that herald any arrival into a modern maternity unit. Protesting with loud cries, the baby would be suddenly quietened by the mother's smile.

A vague memory would stir, an echo of a voice whispering -
"... no matter who is wearing it

⇥24⇤

It was an early Easter that year, and the usual get-together of the two families was due to take place at the Hall. The Easter egg hunt, either in the gardens, or inside the large house if the weather was poor, was now an annual family tradition eagerly anticipated by the two older children. Lucy, as ever, was boasting to the latest au pair that she knew where absolutely all of the eggs were hidden and no-one else would get even one – she would feed them all to Mindy the puppy who, now five months old, large and boisterous, was proving to be a real handful.

Vicky overheard, shuddered at the thought of the awful effects too much chocolate might have on both child and dog, but decided not to intervene. It was her way of coping with both her daughter and her husband these days, and if it meant that both were given full rein with their selfishness, at least it meant that she had some sort of peace. Vicky had discovered something of the art of her late mother-in-law – of ignoring the things that would cause her too much trouble to solve. Sonia, of course, had gone on to refine this art by only getting involved with things that would bring her rewards – especially the personal satisfaction of being in control of other people's lives. That particular refinement lingered in the air over Victoria, with a faint question mark. Time would tell.

Richard telephoned that evening to let Ben and Victoria know that Jaqui had started labour and he would be in touch the following morning to let her know about the baby. The plan was to be that his parents, who were already at home taking care of Tim and Ella, would take the older children to hospital to visit their new brother or sister, then he would like to bring them over to the

171

Hall as usual, as they were so looking forward to seeing Lucy and telling her about the new baby. Victoria agreed, hoping that it might make Lucy more amenable to the thought of her own imminent brother or sister.

Easter Saturday 2007 dawned, with Jaqcueline still in hospital but with nothing happening.

"False labour" the midwife pronounced. "It happens sometimes. I'll get the doctor to see you and make a decision."

Richard tried to soothe her worries, but not for the first time felt thankful that his own professional training gave him the knowledge that could comfort his wife. He telephoned his parents, then the Hall. Returning to the ward he found she was tired and anxious, but seemed to accept his reassurances and lapsed into an uneasy sleep. He knew she would need this for whatever outcome lay ahead, and continued to sit at her side holding her hand.

Easter Sunday afternoon was bright and sunny. Ben had taken Lucy to Church to show off her new dress, leaving Victoria to stay at home at this late stage of her pregnancy, and greet Richard's parents and the children when they arrived for lunch. Lucy returned too full of excitement to eat lunch, and feeling sick because of the sweets that her father had bribed her with during the service. It was not a good omen. Victoria saw the afternoon stretching ahead relentlessly, without even the comfort of a reassuring chat with Jacqui to look forward to.

Muriel and Ted, Richard's parents, had arrived with Tim and Ella, who were bearing small gifts for Lucy. When she came back from church with her father she tossed them aside without even opening them and unable to contain herself any longer announced that the treasure hunt must start *right now*!

"Anything for a bit of peace" said Victoria as she told the children they should join in before Lucy found all the eggs. Soon, shrieks and calls let the adults know that it was indeed under way. It was pleasant enough sitting on the patio in that warm forerunner of Spring that sometimes comes early in the year. Ben, Victoria, Muriel and Ted (Tim and Ella's grandparents) relaxed with drinks, making small talk before lunch. The older couple were naturally anxious about the news from the hospital, but hid their feelings from their hostess.

The three cousins usually played well together, but without Jacqui's calming influence and gift for sensing trouble before it even started, coupled with Victoria's leniency verging on indifference, disaster was inevitable. Lucy overstepped the mark when she pushed Ella off the terrace in full view of all the adults. Ben's patience snapped. He picked up his daughter bodily and carried her to her room kicking and screaming, beating at his back with her small fists.

Flinging her on the bed, he pinned her down by the shoulders and shouted at her to learn to behave like a Woolston, not like her mother, and never, *ever*, to let him down in front of visitors again. His distorted face was only inches away from her terrified gaze – the normally loving, indulgent father had been replaced by someone she couldn't recognise. Her world was shattered; hysterical sobs shook her small body, but Ben ignored them.

He abruptly left the room, slamming the door and turning the key, leaving his daughter to cope with her feelings - alone and unloved.

The embarrassment of Ben's reaction outweighed any effect of Lucy's behaviour. Tim comforted Ella, the adults made the best of things and lunch was eventually over, leaving Muriel and Ted to drive their two grandchildren home as soon as was decently possible, with assurances that they would pass on any news about Jacqui as soon as they heard from Richard at the hospital.

Ben retreated to the Library as soon as they had left, giving instructions that as he had the key to Lucy's room, he would be the one to decide when she would be released. Two hours later, fuelled by misery and brandy, his fury was soon rekindled by another plea from his wife, made as he prepared to go upstairs.

Possibly anything would have had the same effect, but Victoria voiced it, and therefore was on the receiving end of yet another tirade from her husband. She wept, and retreated to the conservatory where, horrified, she realised that she was feeling the early signs that her own labour had started. With barely time to comfort her daughter, now released from her room and delivered into the care of the au pair, she told Ben. He made her wait while he resentfully drank a strong coffee, then wordlessly carried her bag to the car and drove to the hospital.

✂

It was a miserable start that carried a heavy foreboding about the future – their future as a couple, the future of the child as yet unborn, and most definitely the unknown future of their emotionally damaged daughter Lucy who would always carry the entwined memory of the shame of her own actions, betrayal by the person she loved most, abandonment by all those others in her life, linked with the toppling of her priority in the family structure.

⇥25⇤

THIS TIME OF COURSE, BEN had actually managed to bring himself to attend the birth – resentfully and sulkily. When he realised it was another girl he left the delivery room, feigning faintness. Later, he returned to the bedside with flowers, but no improvement in his reaction.

"You can't even get *this* right" he glowered. "*Another* girl, would you believe." His disappointment could not be concealed, and there was no sign of tenderness – either towards his wife or his new daughter.

Victoria shrank into the pillows of her private bed. Such unfair comments at a time like this – she would make him pay dearly when she recovered, and there would certainly be no more attempts to produce a son and heir. She turned her head away from his perfunctory kiss and, glad of any excuse to get him out of the room, soothed the baby's fractiousness.

In the other hospital, Richard leaned over and carefully stroked their son's cheek. Now several hours old, he looked more normal with the tubes removed, and Jacqui had been able to feed him. It had turned out to be a difficult delivery, with cause for concern at first with the baby, who had problems breathing immediately after his birth. Richard had held his wife close and stroked her hair while the staff bustled about the room.

"You'll be able to hold him soon. They've just put him in the incubator for a few hours as a precaution. It happens with many babies and he'll be fine. He looks absolutely gorgeous – you've given me a son to be proud of."

He kissed her tenderly and waited for her to drift off into sleep before going to see the gynaecologist, dreading what he knew from his medical training would be the likely outcome of the conversation.

"Not enough oxygen… possible risk of brain damage … only time will tell."

There would be the question mark of other long-term effects hanging over them for many years to come, Richard knew, but his trained eye had been able to pick out the early tell-tale signs, and the consultant's words had confirmed the prognosis. Jaqui's eyes held the question as he returned – Richard did not need to give the answer in words, but as they held hands and drank in every detail of the soft little features, Jacqui cradled him to her heart, murmuring "Whatever you're capable of, little one, we'll help you achieve it."

They planned that when Richard had collected Tim and Ella and they were all safely back at home as a family, they would explain to the children how special their little brother was and how he would need extra love from all of them.

"Have you phoned Ben?"

"I was saving the news – Vicky went into labour, and you know how short that can be with a second baby – she had another daughter just before midnight last night! Mother and baby are doing just fine."

"Oh Richard! I do hope Ben's pleased. It will be lovely to have two cousins sharing the same birthday and growing up together. I hope we can see much more of them and help little Lucy to feel she's part of a big family."

Jacqui's optimism never seemed to fade, and Richard loved her for that willingness to aim at the best possible outcomes. He knew that no matter what challenges lay ahead, their own son would be cherished and helped to achieve even his smallest successes in an atmosphere of love and support.

The two cousins met for the first time at their joint christening ceremony, just a few weeks after their birth. Tiny morsels of life, with so much in front of them and so many hidden depths acquired through many other lifetimes. What had they come to learn, these little ones, Jacqui wondered. What purposes had they chosen? What were the challenges that lay ahead for all of them as these little lives unfolded?

Victoria and Jacqui posed for photographs, with husbands and children, on the terrace, in the late Spring warmth. Looking at the magnificent surroundings, new growth in the trees, early Summer flowers pushing through the soil, even Victoria became tearful for a moment.

"I do wish your mother was here – just so she could know," she murmured wistfully.

"Something makes me think she is" was Jacqui's response, as the babies touched hands.

✧26✧

THE CELESTIAL REALMS OF THE Afterlife contained an air of celebration as an Angel messenger arrived, with a scroll to be treasured.

> *Memo to Angel Prince of the East (Mr Fu):*
> *Well done, thou good and faithful servant –*
>
> **GOD**

Epilogue

SONIA'S CHOICE IS MADE IN the light of the lessons her soul guides have helped her set for her next life. It has immense impact on all of her family, whatever she has chosen, and the ripples will spread. There is no right or wrong, no easy or difficult – just different opportunities – as there are for us all. The choices she makes in the next earth life will determine how she masters her lessons.

A personal note to the reader:-

Your beliefs may or may not tally with mine, but I hope the tale of
Sonia has brought some thought-provoking moments ... if you were Sonia,
who would you choose?

I welcome any reader's comments. Contact me on:-

lyz.harvey@btinternet.com

Printed in the United Kingdom
by Lightning Source UK Ltd.
120120UK00001B/319-324